THE FAE ARTIFACTOR

Final Book of the Artifactor

HONOR RACONTEUR

Raconteur House

Endless Sea

Kitra Isle

Shera Forest

Whitehaven
Trdnag
Aslinger River
Conger
Jubelirer
Revel
Holly Springs

Jeren Port
Dewall
Zinni River
Herlevi
Greenwell

Ocean Woods
Capson
Hosking

Boscareno
Aszabell
Torgerson

Cavin
Desolate Mountain

The Wasteland

Kindin

Standor Mountains

Mudlands

Tavaris
Chasfin
Slayden

Noppers Woo

Skelton
Gaynah Sea
Louden
Guide
Nakasone

Aeor
Juers
Izus Sea
Haixi

Beyal Lapidoth
Chandra

Hisea Gulf
Appleby
Sea of Grass

Mian Siem
Asheia
Bavelas
Ale

Ramseys River
Briones

Stornaway

Trexler Zufelt

Missun Se

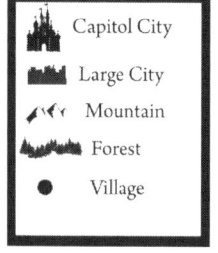

- Capitol City
- Large City
- Mountain
- Forest
- Village

The World of Man

Published by Raconteur House
Murfreesboro, TN

THE FAE ARTIFACTOR
The final book of The Artifactor

A Raconteur House book/ published by arrangement with the author

Copyright © 2019 by Honor Raconteur
Cover by Katie Griffin
Steampunk golden key with mechanical wings on rusty textural background by Black Moon/Shutterstock; ***Three steampunk keys with gears of gold, bronze and steel on black background*** by Black Moon/Shutterstock; ***Fractal smoke swirl*** by Martin Capek/Shutterstock

This book is a work of fiction, so please treat it like a work of fiction. Seriously. References to real people, dead people, good guys, bad guys, stupid politicians, companies, restaurants, cats with attitudes, events, products, dragons, locations, pop culture references, or wacky historical events are intended to provide a sense of authenticity and are used fictitiously. Or because I wanted it in the story. Characters, names, story, location, dialogue, weird humor, and strange incidents all come from the author's very fertile imagination and are not to be construed as real. No, I don't believe in killing off main characters. Villains are a totally different story.

All rights reserved.
No part of this book may be reproduced, scanned, or distributed in any printed or electronic form without permission. Please do not participate in or encourage electronic piracy of copyrighted materials in violation of the author's rights.
Purchase only authorized editions.

For information address: www.raconteurhouse.com

Arandur of South Woods had been a Tracker for many, many years. He knew how to hunt any sort of game, how to track down a lost child, how to search for things not visible to the human eye. He had decades of experience under his belt and knew how to keep his head cool and calm, even as emotions pitched and roiled within him.

When Sevana failed to arrive on time, he didn't immediately panic. Her magic was still unstable; of course she could be delayed. He'd not been able to go with her to the Unda, but his undersea cousins had assured him that they would help her start the craft so that she might be able to fly back without trouble. Still, unforeseen events could have occurred.

An hour passed, and he still didn't panic, although he did pick up the Caller and try to reach her. When that failed, he frowned, the first inkling of doubt rearing its ugly head. Leaving Sevana's study, he went instead to her workroom, finding the largest mirror there and tapping the glass gently with a forefinger. "Milly?"

The spectral woman appeared in a few minutes, her round face creased in a welcoming smile. "Arandur."

"I'm glad you're here," he greeted with relief. Sometimes she visited her children and grandchildren, staying about in Sa Kao. While she could hear someone call her name from great distances, it did take a while for her to get back in the right region and trace which mirror the call came from. "I'm a little worried about Sevana. She was due in an hour ago."

Milly and Sevana had become rather close friends over the past several months. The matron grew visibly concerned. "You're never one to make mountains over mole hills. You're sure she didn't just have trouble starting her flying device?"

Shaking his head, Arandur explained, "The Unda swore they would start it for her. She called me seven hours ago and said she was on her way. Unless something unforeseen has gone wrong, I can't imagine what's delayed her."

"I'll try calling for her." Milly disappeared in the next instant, off to whatever reflective surface she thought would be near her friend. Sevana now kept a mirror on *Jumping Clouds* for the sole purpose of having a backup way to reach home if she fried a Caller. Milly knew exactly which mirror to aim for.

Rocking back on his heels, Arandur set himself to patiently wait. And wait.

They really had to sort Sevana's magic out soon. Arandur knew her to be very frustrated, constantly fighting to do the simplest of spells. He shared her frustration, as this was not what he'd intended when he'd put his blood in her, but then, he hadn't thought of far-reaching consequences at the time. He'd been desperate to save her, nothing else. Now Sevana was this hybrid of Fae and human, her magic core completely disarrayed. No one was sure how to fix her, either.

It would mean a great deal of travel, time, investigation, and patience, but Arandur was of the opinion that they needed to stop Sevana's business and focus on sorting her out. Sevana agreed. The Unda had made some noise about a project they wanted her help on, but Sevana had been firm before going down. She'd bring them children, but any other projects needed to wait until her magical core was fixed. Whatever the Unda wanted would have to wait until later.

They already planned to start with one of Aranhil's contacts. Not that the Fae king actually liked the idea of finding some sort of balance. He much preferred that Sellion become full Fae and come properly home to South Woods. However, Arandur did not think Sevana was ready to cut her ties to the human world just yet.

Aranhil and Sevana hadn't argued about this, but Arandur could see the argument building. It was a question of 'when,' not 'if.'

Milly snapped back to the mirror so hard it nearly cracked the surface. "Arandur! She's not in flight. She's nowhere near *Jumping Clouds.*"

Grabbing the mirror's frame, he focused intently on her. "What exactly did you see? Hear?"

"I didn't hear anything," she denied, visibly agitated and vibrating in place. "But *Jumping Clouds* is in a storeroom of sorts, a huge room made with grey bricks. There's a great many magical artifacts stacked on shelves all around it. Sevana's nowhere in sight."

A place with magical artifacts collected? Arandur's mind sped through the possibilities. Who could possibly catch Sevana mid-flight? Or had they caught her before she could properly get off the ground? Had she crashed? There were too many possibilities. "Did this look like an organized place? Or something cluttered and jumbled, like a looter's storeroom—"

She cut him off with a sharp shake of the head. "Very organized, everything labelled. Not a looter's treasure room. There's a tag near the steering wheel that reads 'Cope Research Foundation, Entry 4863.'"

Alright, that gave him a better idea of what was going on. Some organization had hold of her. The name vaguely rang a few bells for Arandur but he felt like it was something that Sevana had mentioned in passing; he had no knowledge of the place itself. "Tell me about *Jumping Clouds* itself. Does it look damaged? Do you believe she crashed?"

"No, it looks perfectly intact," Milly said, chewing on her bottom lip. "I don't think she crashed. I don't see any other mirrors in that room, but let me try different areas, maybe I can find her. You think she stopped for help and couldn't reach us?"

"It's possible. Things like this have happened before. As long as *Jumping Clouds* didn't crash land, then she's likely not hurt. Keep trying to find her. I'll report this directly to Aranhil and see what Tashjian knows of the place."

She waved him off and Arandur ran from the room to grab the Caller sitting on the table in the study, one of the few surviving in the mountain. Sitting down, he activated it carefully. "Tashjian."

It took a few moments, then the Caller's shape changed into that of Sevana's master, duplicating the same rumpled clothes, messy hairstyle, and disgruntled expression of the old man. From appearances, it seemed that Tashjian had been in the middle of something and it wasn't going well. Arandur recognized that look from Sevana, as she wore it often these days. *"Well, Arandur, what is it? Don't tell me Sevana's melted something again."*

"I'm actually not sure what's wrong," Arandur admitted, trying to phrase this so it wouldn't alarm the other man unduly. "Sevana was due in an hour ago but she hasn't arrived. When Milly checked on her, she found *Jumping Clouds* in what looks to be a storeroom of a place called the Cope Research Institute. Do you know anything about the place?"

Tashjian's irritation shifted into concern, mouth drawing down into a frown. *"I do. But it's out of the way for Sevana, she wouldn't fly over the place. Why is she there?"*

That was indeed the question. "Can you contact them? Do you have a means of doing that?"

"I do. Let me call and see what's happened. And don't panic, I don't think she's been kidnapped. Again."

Snorting, Arandur drawled, "That would be something, to be kidnapped twice in one month. Alright, I'll sit and wait for your word."

"Call you back in a few minutes," Tashjian promised, then the Caller went dormant once more. Thinking that it would be best if he had both communication devices in the same room, Arandur picked up the Caller and headed back to the workroom. He sensed Big's unease and gave the walls a pat as he walked through the hallways. "It's alright. I don't think she's hurt, she's just either had a misadventure of some sort or got sidetracked by some problem. You know how things go with her."

She should be home, Big grumbled back, as discontent as a concerned parent.

Arandur bit back a smile. Big had adopted Sevana as a daughter of sorts years ago and he hadn't changed his stance since. Sevana was his little one that needed protecting, and the best way to do that was to have her under his own roof. "She'll be home, soon enough."

He pulled up a stool in front of the mirror, set the Caller down next to it on its small table, and settled into wait. As he did, he considered different possibilities of what had happened, but the strangeness of her current location didn't make sense. Tashjian was right—if the research institute wasn't anywhere near her flight path home, then how did she get there?

With a snap, Milly popped back into the mirror's image, visibly agitated and moving so much that she rattled the frame of the mirror. "Arandur. I don't like the look of this one bit. I can't get any visual on her, there's not enough reflective surfaces in or out of the building, and the small slivers of reflection that I can use only give me snatches of conversation. I just overhead someone say that 'her magic is too disruptive, either sedate her again or renew the shield on the room.'"

Now he felt alarm, flashing hot and cold, and he straightened from his casual slouch on the stool. How many people had a disruptive magical core right now? What were the odds that someone else was like Sevana? "But you didn't hear anyone use her name?"

"No. I'll keep trying, but…" biting at her lip, Milly confided, "I think it was her they were talking about."

The Caller abruptly came alive with Tashjian's features and he looked fit to be tied. *"Arandur. I've called three different people that I know down there and as soon as they realized it was me, they all immediately ended the call. They looked quite panicked too. I don't know what's going on down there, but I think they have Sevana, and I don't think she's there of her own volition."*

"It appears that way," Arandur agreed, anger building like a steady, roaring fire within him. "Milly overheard a snippet of conversation that makes that very likely. Tashjian, where exactly is this place?"

"Sa Kao, outside of Aleka. Arandur, perhaps we're jumping at shadows."

"If she's grounded in a place outside of her flight route, late without calling anyone, and even Milly can't find her in a place that won't talk to you? Then we're not jumping at shadows," Arandur bit off. "She's being held against her will. Apparently she really can be kidnapped twice in one month. I'm going after her, Tashjian."

Tashjian opened his mouth, ready to argue, then grimaced and bit it back. *"No, you're right, all of that tallied together makes it too conclusive to ignore. But you shouldn't go after her alone. The research institute has some of the finest magicians in the world. They'll put up quite the fight even against one of the Fae."*

The smile that crossed his face was not at all nice. "I never said that I would go alone."

Tashjian looked alarmed. *"Wait, don't call a war party for this! We can call the king of Sa Kao, he might be able to help us."*

"One of ours has been taken. Again. We will not let this go a second time." Done with the conversation, and anxious to be moving, he pushed the stool back and ran through the tunnels and to the back door in Big as quickly as he could move. He could hear both Tashjian and Milly calling after him, but he ignored them. There was nothing else to say at the moment. The mountain shifted with him, his rocks grating in agitation. Arandur patted a wall in reassurance as he moved. "Don't worry. I'll find her."

You always do, Big answered, still clearly worried. *Be safe.*

"Trust me, Big. I'll find her."

Arandur made a new land speed record getting back to the heart of South Woods. He more or less stumbled into Aranhil's meadow, panting and flushed, feeling far more out of breath than he had since a child. In fact, he was so out of sorts that people visibly cut themselves off and stared at him.

Aranhil had been relaxed on his throne but even he straightened, picking up on Arandur's alarm. "What is it, Arandur?"

Striding straight for him, Arandur made the proper bow of greeting, then rattled everything off in rapid fire. "Aranhil. Sevana was taken some hours ago by a facility called the Cope Research Foundation."

The king of the Fae's power stirred in a powerful eddy, sparking in anger. "I am displeased. This world seems to think it can take our daughter as it wishes. This facility, it gave no notice to us?"

"None. Milly was the one who found her location—or I should say, the location of *Jumping Clouds*. At this time, we still have not ascertained where she resides in the facility. I spoke with Tashjian Joles on the way here and he informs me that there is no viable reason for them to take her. This is a magical research facility, one that is well known and respected in Mander. It has no dark motives that we know of."

"That does not ease my mind." Aranhil stood, snapping out his robes as he did so, every fiber of his being bristling like an enraged porcupine. He gestured to people as he moved. "Lock down the defenses. Mothers, see to the children, and warriors, with me. We will go to Sellion directly. Arandur, you know of where this Institute is?"

"I do," Arandur answered, baring his canines in a feral expression. He'd not seen that particular look on his king's face in decades and he thrilled to see it now. Blood would spill this day.

Word spread quickly, Aranhil's command covering all of South Woods within minutes. The very trees sang of a call to arms, the air shaking with the bloodlust that rose. Arandur stopped at his house just long enough to switch weapons, to take on the powerful claymore that he rarely used, then joined the others waiting on the edge of their eastern border. Aranhil had changed from his flowing robes into something imminently practical, a set of armor made of dwarven chainmail and sturdy leathers. He went completely unarmed, however—at least, to the visible eye. Arandur knew better than to take that visual state as truth.

With everyone gathered on their chellomi, the Fae army moved seamlessly forward. Arandur rode stirrup to stirrup with Aranhil for one reason only—he was the only one among them who knew where to go. Six hundred warriors rode behind him in a thunderous wave of hooves. Aside from the jangling of harnesses and the reverberations of the earth, the party moved in eerie silence. No one needed to speak or ask questions. They only had one goal in mind: Rescue their taken sister. Destroy those foolish enough to take her.

They rode. And rode. The chellomi's hooves barely touched the earth, covering great distances with each stride, golden manes and tails streaming in the wind. They did not tire, or strain, their movements poetry itself as they covered miles and leagues without truly noticing the distance. They passed settlements and towns, villages and farms. The humans came out to see what the commotion was, then stared in awe at their passing. Never in living memory had the Fae nation moved en-masse like this. They watched with first amazement, then growing terror, as they recognized a war party on the hunt.

And none of them knew the target.

The war party crossed the borders into Sa Kao without notice or care, as human borders meant little to them. The coast of the Missun Sea was their goal, and the building outside of Aleka—the Cope Research Institute. Arandur led them directly there, across the Sea of Grass, a flat land that gave no trouble to the chellomi's stride. It took barely seven hours to cross the distance, and they arrived as the moon rose into the sky, the sun settling into its bed beyond the horizon.

Arandur had been in Aleka a few times before, so he knew the general layout of the city. They avoided its main roads, splitting off to the right toward the two-lane highway that led to the more industrial section of the city. Even at this time of night, their passing did not go unnoticed, and people's doors and windows popped open to see what the noise was. One good look, and they frantically shut them again, calling out warnings to their families and neighbors to stay inside. The close quarters of the buildings on either side of the road made it easy to hear them, even over the loud ringing of so many hooves on paved stone, and Arandur's mouth quirked in a humorless twitch. The citizens of Aleka need not worry.

They were not the target.

Bypassing the last of the houses, the war party reached the fenced-in area of the Institute's grounds. The research institute had sectioned off quite a bit of space around their buildings, perhaps as a safety precaution to the rest of the city, as they probably had accidents like Sevana did. Accidents that resulted in explosions.

To a Fae's eyes, the darkness posed no problem, and Arandur saw clearly ahead of them. Across the flat, manicured lawn stood the Institute itself, a four-story building made of red sandstone. It sprawled out in every direction, with a very large building peeking out from behind the flat roofline in the back, obviously a warehouse for storage. Arandur supposed that *Jumping Clouds* was housed in there. But his purpose was retrieving its creator, not the creation, after all. He paid the building no mind for now.

The fence was made of the same sandstone as the building. It represented no obstacle, as a wave of Aranhil's hand flattened it to dust, allowing the chellomi across without even breaking stride.

Perhaps they'd somehow been alerted the Fae were coming, although Arandur didn't know how. Sevana, perhaps. No matter the reason, the building blazed with light from floor to ceiling, people scurrying about with torches in their hands, shouting at each other. Arandur could not pick out the words and did not try to. He kept his eye on Aranhil—they all did—as their king stopped midway across the yard. Staying astride his chellomi, Aranhil lifted a hand and gestured sharply.

With a groan of protest, the building rent in twain right down the center.

If there had been calls of alarm amongst the building's occupants before, it didn't compare to now, as they screamed in panic and terror. Some of them were knocked off their feet, forced to catch themselves on the edge of the floor before they fell three stories to the bottom. Others huddled against the walls, peering out frantically to try and divine the source.

"Tracker," Aranhil commanded in glacial tones. "Find our daughter."

Arandur immediately sprang off his chellomi and loped forward. He made it ten feet before several men in white coats, wands in hand, dared to block his way. His hand automatically rose for the sword strapped to his back, but Arandur didn't do more than get his hand around the hilt before several of his brothers and sisters called upon the earth to wrap the magicians up in grass and dirt, locking them into above-ground coffins. Not bothered, Arandur continued on his way, searching with every sense for any sign of Sevana.

Being a Tracker meant more than knowing how to read the prints and impressions of a person's passing in the earth. Every soul left an afterimage of itself in the world, a sense that the eyes could not see, but that Arandur could detect. It was a combination of magic, senses honed and trained to be sensitive, and an instinctual understanding of what he searched for. Sometimes he didn't need to strain overmuch to find a trail, as normal eyesight and knowledge of tracking was sufficient.

This time, he used every ounce of skill, every bit of knowledge he knew of Sevana. Nothing in this area spoke of her presence. Dark brows drawing into a frown, he moved further into the building, hearing the creaks and groans as the frame protested, knowing that it had moments before parts of it would fall through. Some people were hurt, crying for help, others huddled under their personal shields, staring at him with wide eyes white with fear. He ignored all, found a hallway still intact, and stormed several feet inside the formerly pristine white building. Nothing.

Perplexed and growing worried, Arandur backtracked to the opposite half of the building, moving now at a faster lope, nearly a full out run. People streamed past him in the opposite direction, this lot having gotten past their shock and confusion and now trying to leave for the questionable safety of the outside. He ignored them, pushing past when necessary, eyes darting to take in every ounce of space. Sevana. She'd passed through this part of the hallway at some point, hours ago. Her impression in the air faded steadily, but still strong enough to see.

Arandur followed it directly to a room, the door of which had been wrenched open, and he stood for a second within the frame, staring at the empty bed inside, the chair knocked over to its side. She'd lain on that bed for a few hours, no more, then something else had taken her. Something with a strong magical signature. Unda? No.

Someone who had made recent contact with the Unda. He detected the scent of the sea and his underwater cousins.

What did that mean? Did the Unda realize what had happened to her? Had they pursued her here somehow, sent someone to rescue her and fetch her to safety again? If so, why not communicate that with Aranhil?

With an ill feeling clenching up his chest, Arandur backed out of the room, intent on reporting this to his king first before catching onto the trail and following it out. This time he did sprint, making it out of the crumbling building's edge and onto the grass before slowing again.

A powerful magician faced Aranhil, a wand clenched in his hand, although he was smart enough to keep it facing down and at his side. The man looked older, perhaps in his fifties, his salt-and-pepper hair standing on end, every fiber of his being screaming of outrage and alarm. As Arandur closed in on his back, the man remained oblivious, arguing heatedly with Aranhil. "—no cause to come and attack us like this! I demand an answer from you, and for you to restore this building to rights!"

Aranhil caught his eye and motioned with a jerk of the chin to the man. Arandur did not need the hint. Sneaking up, he snapped the wand out of the man's hand with his right even as his left pulled free a dagger and slid it to the front of the man's throat. The magician in his grasp froze, a strangled noise of air leaving his throat, breath stuttering in panic.

Pressed against the man's back, Arandur leaned his mouth near the man's ear and asked in a low, guttural tone, "Where is Sellion?"

"She is not within the building?" Aranhil demanded, and the war party behind him snarled in growing anger. The chellomi were equally vexed, stamping their hooves and tossing their heads with angry snorts.

"She is not," Arandur answered, never taking his eyes off the man in his grasp. "She was, as of three hours ago, but no longer. Another man who smells of the sea came to take her. I saw traces of Unda on the man. I can track them, of course, but I want an answer as to why they took her to begin with, and what happened. Answer me, magician. Where is our sister?"

"W-we," the magician started on a gasp, then paused to swallow before managing, "we haven't taken a Fae woman. We wouldn't dare."

"Sellion," Arandur repeated, a cold suspicion worming through his mind. "You would know her by her human name—Artifactor Sevana Warren."

The magician went abruptly still in Arandur's grasp. "What?"

"She is our daughter," Aranhil pressed, urging his chellomi closer, his aura alive with anger like a live bonfire. "Adopted by us because of her kindness, bonded to us further by Fae blood. You will tell me why you took her, why you gave us no notice of your designs upon her, and then you will tell us who took her from this place."

Arandur judged the man ready to pass out any second and debated on whether to move the knife closer to the jugular or further away. Sevana would say further away. He wasn't in the right frame of mind to consider this man's death a waste, however. In fact, he rather thought of it more like a benefit to the world. "W-we had to take her in. Her magic was flaring wildly out of control, causing magical eddies and malfunctions; it was o-our only recourse, an-and—"

"She was attempting to find help to stabilize her magic," Arandur crooned near the man's ear, his lip curling upwards in a barely contained snarl. He noticed the nervous sweat pouring off the man and ignored it. Arandur did not care if this man were so terrified he were close to wetting himself. He wanted answers. "You did a foolish thing."

"You'll be punished for that shortly," Aranhil informed the magician. His expression settled into an icy calm, not unlike the sky before a mother storm rolled in. "But answer the other question. Where has she gone?"

"We don't know," the man rasped out. "We were searching the grounds before you came. She was in her room two hours ago, we all know that she was, and then suddenly she wasn't. We're not sure how she got out. But she couldn't have done it under her own power and she took nothing of hers with her. P-please you have to believe me, if we'd known of her ties to you, we'd never have taken her, we were just trying to contain her magic before she did any further damage and—"

Arandur grew tired of the man's pleading and roughly clocked him on the back of the head with the hilt of his dagger. The magician promptly passed out, thudding in an untidy splay of limbs on the grass. Without any concern for him, Arandur stepped aside, avoiding the limp body. "Aranhil. I will follow the trail as I can, but if the Unda are behind her rescue, I fear they took her back to the sea."

"If they did so without word to me, I will not be pleased." Aranhil looked over the ground of the place, anger still roiling about him. "Go and confirm her trail as much as you can. We will teach the ones here what it means to take a daughter of the Fae."

"Perhaps remove Sellion's things first," Arandur suggested lightly, then gave a quick bow before loping off again. He'd need to pick up the trail quickly and leave the area in the next minute. The war party behind had been denied blood and the return of their sister. They would not take that well.

Arandur found the trail, followed it out of the building, then whistled for his chellomi. It was as if that whistle was all the signal the war party needed. He barely had his foot in the stirrup when the two halves of the main building crashed into the ground at such velocity that an earthquake couldn't begin to compete. Someone better have retrieved Sevana's things.

There wouldn't be anything standing before the night was out.

1

Sevana had not been truly awake for the past few hours, as the magicians of the research institute had put her under a sedative spell in order to contain her. Not that she could do much without any tools to work with, but their precautions had been wise, as she had been desperate enough to use her explosive magic to melt the door off its hinges and try running for it. Sevana had only felt a brief flash of concern for herself—she didn't think anyone at the research institute would actually hurt her—but mostly for the city that surrounded them. When her Fae family finally figured out where she was, they would not respond kindly, to say the least.

So when her 'rescuers'—she wasn't sure they actually should be called that—came calling, Sevana's senses were fuzzy and she had no ability to focus. She smelled the salt and brine of the sea, felt cool skin as they lifted her out of the bed, only vaguely aware of their passage as they left behind white walls for the open darkness of the outside. As much as she struggled to focus, it was beyond her; she could only wait for the spell to fade.

They reached the shoreline, and after that it was a blur of dark water, movement, and the gentle lights of schools of glow fish whirling around them. Sevana unwittingly slept—she must have—as the next time her eyes opened, the spell had dissipated. Her focus had returned, leaving her in control again of her body.

Great dark magic, but did she ever hate sedative spells.

It took a single glance for her to realize where she was. Not that she'd ever been in this particular room before, but it didn't take a genius to figure it out. The walls were smooth and cold, like the sea, made of a stone not unlike a cave and threaded with calcite, the mineral fluoresce giving off a dim glow of illumination. Sevana lay stretched out on a bed of woven fabric, much like a hammock, with linens no doubt purchased from the shore. Or salvaged from sunken ships. It smelled strongly of the ocean down here, and she could hear through the walls the sounds of others moving about, talking, and the clatter of feet upon sea stone. This absolutely must be one of the guest quarters with the Unda, probably of Living Waters. Sevana estimated she had only been unconscious a few hours, so her captors wouldn't have had the time to take her to some other clan's territory. Living Waters was the only possibility.

And she'd just left them this morning, so why bring her back here?

If they had somehow discovered her kidnapping, that was all well and fine, but why bring her back into their territory? Waiting on Aran to come fetch her? Sevana really wanted to believe the best of their intentions, but unfortunately, she knew the king and queen of this nation all too well. They were not known for being altruistic.

Grumbling to herself, she swung her legs over the side of the bed and headed for the door, yanking her shirt back into order as she moved. Aran was absolutely going to have kittens over this. So would Master. She wouldn't be able to go anywhere for months without someone shadowing her.

Sevana had a single toe out of her doorway when someone shifted to block her. She looked up into the eyes of Taslim, the guard in charge of the southern border, looking as big and bulky as always. Over his shoulder she caught a glimpse of the outside and realized she really was in one of the guest houses, in the section of the town meant for outlanders, as a large protective canopy that provided air and dry ground surrounded the building. It allowed her to stand toe-to-toe with him on dry ground, as he had shed his half-mermaid form for two legs, likely so he could escort her. "Taslim."

"Artifactor," he greeted her with mock pleasantness. "You are awake. We are glad."

"Not for long, you won't be," she promised him darkly. His grin widened, showing sharpened canines. The Unda loved people who put up a good fight. "Taslim, I would speak with either Curano or Rane."

"Our honored queen awaits you," he assured her brightly. "Rane has much to discuss with you and only waited for you to awaken. I am to escort you."

That mollified her only some. Rane no doubt had an agenda up her sleeve, and Sevana didn't like not knowing what that was. "Fine. Lead on."

Taslim led the way for her along the sea floor. This section of the city butted up against the outside sea wall, looking entirely majestic—every coral reef groomed to within an inch of its life, schools of fish moving about like a living painting. The lighting was warm and somewhat dim here, the deepness of the water keeping natural sunlight out, and the fluorescent minerals in the walls of the rounded buildings offset the gloom. More oval-shaped florescent lights hung here and there to keep the city well lit. It was much like walking through a large, wide cave tunnel with the mixture of dimness and glowing lights, a beautiful if somewhat eerie experience. Sevana truly felt like she'd fallen into a large aquarium, an impression reinforced by the conical shape of the buildings. They spread out around her like a small city, something a bit larger than Milby, perhaps? She had no real sense of size, as she could barely see any real distance because of the twists and turns of the roads blocking her view.

Sevana saw quite a few of the Unda moving about, most of them choosing their full forms as seals as they moved, others remaining in a half-half state. Hands were easier to use than flippers, after all. She also caught glimpses through open doors of the children she'd brought the day before, already engaging shyly with new parents, their bodies just starting the process of adapting to Unda magic. A few spied her, lighting up and waving. Despite herself, she waved back.

"We are very happy with our children," Taslim informed her as they strolled along. "They are shy, but good children. They ask many questions, which relieves us, as there is much for them to learn."

Seeing an opportunity to get some information out of him, Sevana pressed, "Is that why I was brought back here? To negotiate more children?"

"We always welcome children," Taslim answered frankly, "but that is not why our monarchs had you brought back here. You required aid. I was watching from the shore to make sure that you lifted in the air properly on your device and saw you captured instead. We rescued you and brought you here, as it was the only safe place to retreat to."

That all sounded well and good, but she sensed an ulterior motive under the surface. There were only two reasons why people wanted Sevana. They either wanted her to fix something or they needed something built. That didn't surprise her much, but the timing of it seemed suspicious. Rane and Curano both knew that her magic was out of whack, so why would they ask her to solve a problem for them? There wasn't much she could do about anything just now. Was she looking a gift horse in the mouth? Were they really only here because it was a safe place to go, to protect her until help could arrive?

Sevana had no time for further questions, as they'd apparently reached the 'throne room,' or at least a grand receiving room of some sort. It was a round building like every other building in this city, although larger than the others she'd passed on the street. If such narrow, crooked, switchback pathways between the rocks could be labelled 'streets.' There was little in this room aside from benches that curved along the edges, a thick rug on the floor, and a low dais on the far room. Curano, the Unda King, was not present. Rane, however, lounged about the back of a very large sea turtle, sneaking him tidbits from a plate resting on a pedestal nearby. She was in her fully human form, looking only mildly wet for once, her seafoam green dress lying about her in ruffles, dark hair damp and loosely braided to hang over one shoulder. Rane looked up at their entrance with a smile that she no doubt meant to be welcoming. To Sevana, that many pointed teeth in a single mouth looked alarming.

"Sevana," she greeted happily. "You rose quickly. Excellent."

"Yes, fortunately," Sevana agreed, coming to a stop just in front of the sea turtle. She knew the bite strength of those creatures and carefully stayed out of range of its mouth. "Rane, what is this about?"

"We rescued you," Rane responded with a pout.

"You rescued me, and I'm grateful, and yet I'm here when you should have contacted Aranhil and arranged for a pickup." Sevana crossed both arms over her chest and stared the queen down. "And I know you. You don't do favors for free. So, why am I here?"

"There is a problem I would have your assistance on," Rane informed her casually. "I had you retrieved for this purpose."

"What is this, kidnap me month?" Sevana demanded of the Unda. "First idiot deities, then the Institute, now you lot. And do you have a death wish? You realize Aranhil has absolutely no sense of humor about me, right?"

Rane, Queen of Living Waters, did not look worried about igniting her cousin's ire. She lounged quite casually on the back of a sea turtle, idly stroking the beast's neck and sending it into raptures. "It is fine. You needed rescuing; he'll be lenient in view of that."

Sevana rubbed at her forehead, feeling a headache brewing. Rane had badgered her earlier, as she'd been unloading the kids, about a problem that only she could solve. Sevana had barely paid any attention to her, as she didn't want another project until her magical core was straightened out. She'd promised to help later, if they couldn't solve the problem on their own. She now had the heavy suspicion that Rane would use this situation to force Sevana to help her now. "When I was down here with the kids, you said you had a problem you wanted my help on. But as I told you then, there's no way that I can help sort any problem you have right now."

"And yet you solved the issue with my cousin's territory at Nanashi Isle in your state," Rane argued somewhat mockingly. "This is no different."

Letting her head fall back, Sevana prayed for patience. It spectacularly failed to come. Had they really sent someone after her, rescued her, and then decided that while they had her, they might as well use her? That smelled, and it wasn't fried chicken. She'd likely regret asking, but couldn't seem to help herself. "And what, pray tell, is this aid that you need?"

"We have a problematic issue with our transport system for you to solve," Rane informed her.

Ah, regret. You came so soon. "Rane, you do remember that my magical core is out of whack, right?"

"I don't require memory, I can see it clearly even now." Rane sounded very unsympathetic to this situation, her hand waving negligently to indicate Sevana as a whole. "We'll naturally fix that first. I believe the fault is with the Fae blood. It's proven to be incompatible with your blood. We'll do better to make you Unda."

Alarm shot through Sevana. Unda?! No. Most adamantly, emphatically no. She absolutely did not want to spend the rest of her life under the ocean. She did not like salty water, and raw fish made her gag. Her brain skipped through that flash of alarm and rationally pointed out that Rane's statement had nothing to do with magical properties. The Unda's blood quality wouldn't be any different than a Fae's. A variation of it, certainly—the properties wouldn't completely align, otherwise the Fae would have gills and fins. Still, not magically different enough to make a difference in turning a human Other.

With that rational, logical thought in her mind, Sevana calmed enough to say sarcastically, "Uh-huh. Tell you what, Rane. You run that logic by Aranhil and, if he agrees, I'm your girl."

The queen's hand paused in stroking the turtle, lips pressing into a flat line. She clearly didn't expect Sevana to argue that point. "You have no wish to join us?"

"I'm already promised elsewhere." Sevana was proud of herself for such a diplomatic answer. Who said she couldn't play nice when she wanted to? Although if Rane pulled another stunt like this, she'd stop pulling her punches. Sevana might not have much in the way of control at the moment, but the one reliable thing her magic could do these days was make things explode.

Rane openly pouted. "But I like you, Sevana."

"I'm flattered," Sevana answered dryly. "Do you like me enough to start a war? 'Cause you'll get one if you don't call Aranhil soon and reassure him that I'm alright and with you."

A little miffed, Rane stared her down. Sevana met her eyes levelly. Strangely enough, even though the Unda were frankly terrifying, she felt no fear. Sevana was a proven ally of the Unda, a daughter of the Fae, and she knew Rane didn't want to upset her. Or kill her. That gave Sevana a great deal of leeway. She was not above using it.

Very grudgingly, Rane admitted, "I have attempted to send a message to Aranhil. I have not received a response."

Sevana's hindbrain shot out the logistics and the time; when the obvious reason hit her, she winced. "Let me guess. He thinks I'm at the Cope Research Institute still and he's already gone off to storm the place, hasn't he?"

"That would be my guess." Rane gave her a bland smile. "Well. This should prove interesting."

"If by 'interesting' you mean 'utter destruction,' you will not be wrong." Sevana sighed, already resigned. And it had been such a nice research facility, too. Hopefully they wouldn't kill everyone and start an international war. Although she couldn't hold out much hope for that, either. "Alright, Rane. I have the feeling we can only send flowers for a grave at this point. What's done is done. I'll send another message to them saying I'm fine and I'm here—" might as well head off another potential war if she could "—and then we'll discuss just what your plan is for straightening my magic out."

"I have no plans of my own," Rane demurred with that secretive, enigmatic smile that made Sevana's blood skitter nervously like a dog circling a bath. "But I have called upon an expert of magic to examine you. I believe she will be able to fix matters."

Having done her own research on the experts, Sevana eyed her suspiciously. The Unda only had one person that she knew of, and no one had been willing to say the man's name. Granted, that didn't mean much, as Sevana barely knew anyone of the Unda, just who she'd met in the past couple of weeks. That they had a female expert as well as a male shouldn't surprise her. "And who is she?"

"Ursilla."

Sevana's eyes went as wide as saucers in her face. Ursilla. The first Mother of the Unda? *That* Ursilla? The one who gave birth to all of the legends, the first Mother to go upon the shore, seduce human men, and all of that? Unable to check the words, Sevana blurted out, "She's still alive?!"

Rane clapped her hands in delight. "You know of her! Excellent, that speeds matters along."

"Of course I know of her, do you know how many legends she's started among the humans? She's famous, the first selkie ever spotted on land. Not that anyone knew she was actually an Unda at the time and just in her selkie form." Sevana pinched the bridge of her nose, hard, letting the mild pain combat her rising emotions. She didn't know whether she felt excited, panicked, or overwhelmed with the idea of coming face to face with a legend. A legend called solely for her benefit, no less.

"She'll be here in the next hour or so," Rane informed her, as if grandmother was coming over for tea. "Go and write your message, then perhaps a change of clothes?"

"Something to eat, too," Sevana requested, resisting the urge to find a flat surface somewhere and bang her head against it. She felt that instinct often when around Rane. If she gave in now, she'd have no head left by the end of the week.

At the idea of food, her stomach gave a petulant rumble. Part of her reaction was surely due to hunger, as she hadn't eaten since... breakfast. Whenever breakfast was. Twelve hours ago? Fourteen? Sevana wasn't entirely sure of the time. It was naturally dark here, this far under the ocean's surface, which skewed her already addled sense of time.

She did know that if she could eat something not raw, get cleaned up, and send a message to Aran before he had kittens, she'd survive the next few hours without killing someone. Blowing out a breath, she whirled and followed Taslim out.

Ursilla of Living Waters was not at all what Sevana expected. Knowing the woman had to be several centuries old, she'd expected an aging and decrepit crone. And certainly, Ursilla showed her age, but she was far from decrepit. Her iron grey hair flowed gently around her head and down to her waist, the wrinkles about her dark eyes and generous mouth gentle and barely perceptible. She moved in human form, her skirts barely an inch off the floor, and the way she moved spoke of fluidity, as if she still walked in water.

Perhaps she was no longer the seductress who took human men as husbands, but she still carried the charm and grace of her early years.

In the hour that it took for Ursilla to arrive, Sevana had eaten, washed, dressed in some borrowed clothes, and written out a very hasty note to be sent to Aranhil. Now she was glad to be in a more amenable frame of mind, as this was definitely a woman that she didn't want to tick off.

Sevana rose to greet her, a part of her thrilled to meet a living legend, the rest of her unsure how this meeting would go. If anyone could figure her out, Ursilla would be the one, so Sevana hoped the woman could provide answers. But if she couldn't—was there anyone in the world who could possibly match this Unda's knowledge and experience? Asking this woman questions strangely felt like gambling, and Sevana didn't care for it.

"Ursilla," Rane greeted happily, like a grandchild happy to see her grandmother. Reaching out with both hands, she placed a kiss on Ursilla's cheeks, one then another, before pulling back with a grin. "You came so quickly."

"Of course I did," Ursilla answered, her voice low and throaty, somewhat creaking with age. "I was curious and we owe this woman a favor, if nothing else. Well, Sellion of South Woods, come and greet me."

Despite her nerves, Sevana had to grin. Why did Ursilla remind her of Baby? Strange notion. It was something to do with the complete confidence she exhibited, the slightly smug tilt to her lips, the smooth carriage of her gait. It all looked definitively feline. Coming forward, she extended both hands, inclining her head to acknowledge this woman's power and position. "Ursilla. You favor me by coming."

Ursilla's dark eyes narrowed thoughtfully as they swept over her. "I choose to remain in good terms with both Aranhil and the woman who brings us children. If that means helping you with this snarled mess going on inside your magic core, so be it. Tell me, which idiot did this to you? Did he not know better?"

Sevana blinked at her. Could she see Aran's blood so clearly that she could tell it was a man's? Or had someone at least given her the basics? Probably the latter. "He did, actually. It was a desperate situation. I was dying and he only had minutes to work with."

"Ah." Ursilla drew the sound out in low, rolling tones, her expression suddenly empathetic and understanding. "That explains much of what I see. I see a Mother has attempted to mitigate it."

"Yes, for all the good that did. Aran was certain that only an expert could help, as nothing of South Woods's lore spoke of a situation like mine. We were intent on visiting various people before someone—" Sevana cast Rane a dirty look "—took it into her head to intervene. You did get that message to Aran, I hope?"

"We sent it," Rane responded, entirely unapologetic and unconcerned as she lounged once again on her sea turtle's back. "We have no way of knowing if it reached him."

If she caused a war, Sevana would smack her arrogant little head.

Strangely, Ursilla also seemed unconcerned and waved this away with a flap of the hand. "Come, sit. I wish to examine you in depth."

That better not involve either teeth or pain. Sevana, despite her reservations, went along with it and sat on a low padded bench nearby, one leg tucked up under another. Ursilla sat in a similar position in front of her, both of her cool hands closing around Sevana's. Her eyes went from head to crotch, then back again, clearly tracing something. Staying perfectly still, Sevana allowed her to look, carefully not holding her breath.

After several long minutes, Ursilla grunted and released her hands. "I see the problem. Fae magic fights for dominance with your human magic. It is like two saltwater crocodiles fighting for the same territory. Neither can exist in the same space. When you try to work your magic, what happens?"

"Either it doesn't do anything at all, or it explodes with an overabundance of power," Sevana answered forthrightly, fascinated to hear this answer. No one had explained it as such to her before, or even known why she wasn't adapting to the Fae blood, but Ursilla could actually see it? "I can't use spells that are sustained at all."

"Yes," Ursilla nodded along, as if what Sevana explained made perfect sense to her. "It is because your magical core doesn't know how to respond when you call to it. Do you want the human magic? The Fae? Sometimes it hesitates, not knowing how to answer you. Sometimes it sends both."

Sevana's head whirled with this information, her own observations about her magic and experiences swirling about until it fell into place, all of the pieces now explained. It made perfect sense. "Ursilla. Are you guessing, or do you actually see this?"

Impishly, the Unda smirked, and for a moment she looked centuries younger. "Oh, I have very good eyes. I can see it. I can also see the problems facing either solution. You have two ways open to you."

Blinking, Sevana regarded her in bemusement. How could she possibly have two? "I'm listening."

"First, we turn you wholly Fae, or as close as we can." Holding up a hand, Ursilla warned, "This will not be a perfect metamorphosis. Your human body is too established for that, your human magic too tightly engrained with your blood. But we can change the majority of you over to Fae, and with that, your human magic will fade. You will exchange it for Fae magic."

The way she explained this gave Sevana the notion that it wasn't her physical body that would fail to become fully Fae. Or at least, not just that. "I won't be able to master Fae magic, will I."

"Not entirely," Ursilla agreed, somewhat apologetically. "You will remain at the level of a child's, perhaps a teenager's ability. But your magic ability as a human was not that of a master either, correct? You are an Artifactor, not a Sorceress."

That…did put things into perspective, didn't it? Sevana had never been powerful with her magic. It was her knowledge, her intuitive creativity, that had carved her path in the magical world. Said like that, the idea of becoming fully Fae didn't seem such a bad choice. Although she'd have to study and figure out how magic worked all over again. Revisiting her student days did not excite her. "You said two options, though. What's the second?"

"I can strip most of the Fae blood from you, reset your human magic to a degree, but I warn you, child. You will not return to how you were. Your human magic will remain unruly and somewhat volatile. You'll just have less trouble managing it." Hesitating, Ursilla added slowly, "And I do not think it will do your physical form much good either. I have only encountered a case like yours twice. Neither of them were magicians, only magic touched, but when I stripped the Unda blood from them, their physical forms aged faster than a human's should. You will not live out your intended lifespan."

Blowing out a steady stream of air, Sevana sat back and looked blankly toward the ceiling, thinking hard and fast. Was it really a choice at all? Die early with magic that still didn't really cooperate, or become fully Fae and figure out magic all over again. While both options had cons, the pros of one far outweighed the other.

Part of Sevana really did not like the idea of becoming Fae. She had so many ties and relations with the human world, and if she became fully Fae, she knew good and well that her new Fae family would not want her to live separate from them. They already worried about her being in Big now. In a sense, she'd be even more vulnerable in the next few years as she relearned magic from the beginning. It would take quite the fight to remain as she was, even for a few years longer, and Sevana did not look forward to it. Not one iota.

And yet, that was truly her only objection. In every other aspect, becoming Fae filled her with anticipation. What would it be like, to see the world as they did? To talk to the elements as her Fae brothers and sisters? Would it not give her the opportunity to see the world not as she perceived it, but as it was? How many Artifactors had dreamed of doing just that?

It would mean slowly losing her human ties, of seeing loved ones die ahead of her, but it would give her another family in return. Really, in the end, there was no other decision to be made.

As her eyes met Ursilla's once more, she knew that the Unda had already known what decision Sevana would make, but she had patiently waited for Sevana to work it out for herself. Then again, anyone who had been alive for centuries would likely have quite the well of patience. "I think the only sane decision is to become fully Fae."

Rane clapped her hands and chortled with outright glee. "I knew you would! But surely, Ursilla, it would be safer to make her Unda."

"Rane," Ursilla reproved mildly, like a grandmother scolding a child for asking for yet another cookie. "No."

Pouting, the Queen of Living Waters crossed her arms over her chest and looked deliberately elsewhere. "You can't blame me for trying."

Ursilla didn't openly roll her eyes, but the expression on her face said she did so on an internal level. Ignoring the pouting queen, she informed Sevana, "We will need the donor of your blood nearby in order to start your transformation. This will take several weeks, I believe. You must call for him."

"Well, as to that," Sevana jerked a thumb towards Rane, "I've already tried. This one is going along with the letter instead of the spirit of the law. Arandur is the one who changed me."

Ursilla grumbled something under her breath that sounded like a very ancient curse, in probably something now considered a dead language. "We will send someone to meet him. Where is he likely to be?"

"On my trail, looking for me," Sevana answered with a sigh. "He likely thinks that I was kidnapped. Again."

Ursilla's thin brows arched at the 'again.' "You are kidnapped often?"

"This seems to be the month for it, for some reason. Anyway, he's likely on the shoreline now, trying to get someone from the Unda to respond to him. Perhaps we should go up and talk to him?" Sevana suggested this casually, hoping that Ursilla would do the honors and neatly outmaneuver Rane at the same time. She knew very well that

Rane did not want her back on shore where Aran or Aranhil could grab her.

Rane squawked in protest. "You must not, Mother!"

"Peace, child, we must do the transformation down here where I can comfortably work with her blood," Ursilla responded, already rising to her feet. "But we must have this Arandur on hand. And if we do not let the King of South Woods see her with his own eyes, we will have quite the war on our hands. I do not care for the idea of putting our new children in danger, do you?"

Flinching at the reproof, Rane muttered something unintelligible.

"She will return," Ursilla promised her, completely unruffled. "Come, Sellion. I will take you to the surface. Let us find your kindred and settle things."

By the time that Sevana's head rose above the waves, she knew that she'd been dead on with her predictions. An entire war party stretched out along the banks, most of them still mounted and bristling with weapons. The night air was brisk and cold, and the water lapped harshly against her wet boots, sending a shiver down her spine and over her skin. Sevana quickly tried to get a head count, but the moonlight wasn't strong enough for her human eyes to penetrate far, and only the glint off platinum blond hair or drawn weapons gave her any clue as to how many Fae warriors were arrayed in front of her.

Aranhil stood on the sand with his boots just touching the water, arguing heatedly with one of the Unda guards. The guard was apologetic, bobbing his head up and down, but adamant in his stance of not escorting the war party below the waves.

Sevana didn't get more than five words out before Aran's head snapped around; when he spied her, he leapt straight into the water. "Sevana!"

She gave an *oof* as he scooped her up, breath knocking out of her lungs as strong arms wrapped around her like steel bands. Awkwardly—her arms were half-pinned—she patted his back. "I'm alright, I'm alright."

"Sellion!" Aranhil also slogged into the water, reaching her side and prying Aran off—not that her friend moved more than six inches. Her king, on the other hand, looked fit to be tied. "Why are you here, daughter?"

"Peace," she soothed him, not wanting war to break out on the spot. "Rane was a bit high-handed with matters, and we've had words about it, but all with good intentions. Her guards saw me taken, one of them tracked me to the research facility, and they staged a rescue. Because they weren't operating under direct orders, they didn't know what else to do, so they brought me back to Living Waters to report in."

Aranhil looked torn between relief and aggravation. "Rane could have said something."

"She did send a message, but I think it passed you on the road," Sevana answered steadily. She was not blind to the fact that both men had a tight grip on her, and knew that they'd been scared badly by her third disappearance. Not that she was precisely happy with it either. Kidnapping left much to be desired. "Ah, do I dare ask what you did to Cope Institute?"

Lifting his nose in a haughty manner, Aranhil informed her, "Such a place took my daughter. Of course they were punished."

Sighing, she went with the more direct question. "Is it still standing?"

"No."

"That figures," she muttered, resigned. Catching sight of Ursilla standing nearby, watching this play out with open amusement, she belatedly remembered her manners. "Aranhil, do you know this esteemed lady?"

Turning, Aranhil regarded the elderly Unda for a long moment, losing his arrogance and becoming slightly more deferential. "I have not had that honor, though I believe I know who she is. Well met, Ursilla."

"Well met, Aranhil of South Woods," Ursilla returned with her throaty voice, giving him a simple inclination of the head in greeting. "As you see, your daughter was safe with us. We would not harm one who belongs to you, nor disregard the many blessings she has given us as our friend."

At that, Aranhil slowly relaxed. "Of course. You must pardon my panic. We have already lost her once due to someone else's arrogance, then again twice in one night. We were beside ourselves with worry."

"I quite understand. However, I must speak with you regarding your daughter." Ursilla drifted closer, the skirt of her dress floating about on top of the ocean waves like decorative sea foam. "I have examined her, and I believe that I know how to fix her."

Everyone within earshot—and that was the entire war party; the Fae had good hearing after all—immediately focused on Ursilla, all ears. Sevana waited with a mix of emotions, as she was glad to finally have a course to follow, a solution in hand, but she just knew that it would start a whole new round of arguments.

"We must turn her wholly Fae, but do so in careful and guarded increments," Ursilla continued without prompting. "She will never be true Fae, in body and magic, but I believe her change will be as complete as a teenager's. She will have good health, a decent lifespan, and her magic will settle into a stabilized nature."

Aranhil lit up, delighted by this news. "We thought a complete change would do so, but we were unsure of the process. You can do this safely?"

"I can," Ursilla confirmed calmly.

He gave her a deep inclination of the head, his long blond hair swinging forward over one shoulder, as close to a bow as Sevana had ever seen him give. "You honor us with your aid, Ursilla. I would be very glad to leave my daughter in your hands."

"I'll be happy to help her, as your daughter is also our friend. But I must have the blood of the one who initially turned her, to help complete the transformation." Her dark eyes turned to Aran and studied him from head to toe. Aran normally stuck out like a sore thumb when standing in a Fae party. His tan skin and thick, unruly dark hair cut short was unlike the rest of them, and his manner of dress was a silent proclamation that he spent most of his time in the human world. Even if Ursilla hadn't been able to see his magical makeup, she would likely have been able to peg him. "This one, I take it."

Aran inclined his torso in an acknowledging bow. "Yes. I am Arandur."

"Ah, Sellion's Arandur," Ursilla responded with understanding, her brow quirked knowingly. "She was quite firm that you would be worried about her. We came up to the surface to find you."

Sevana cleared her throat, fighting a blush. The way Ursilla said this invited everyone else to interpret Sevana's actions in a wholly different way. She hadn't meant it like *that*, Aran was just a very close friend, and he had already been put through the wringer several times in the past two weeks as it was. "Yes, well, I was also concerned there was a war party on his heels. And lookey there, I was correct. Aranhil, Ursilla can fix me, but this will take several weeks, at least, and we'll need Arandur on hand throughout the process."

The quirk in Aranhil's mouth said he'd also caught the insinuation of Ursilla's words, but he let Sevana off the hook and responded to her words instead. "Yes, I imagine this will take time. I also imagine that it would be easiest for Ursilla to work here, within her sea, instead of forcing her to stay up on land. I am correct, Ursilla?"

"You are." Ursilla left it at that, waiting for his response.

He thought for a moment, then his eyes flicked to Aran, still standing so close to Sevana that their sides brushed as they breathed. "You will go with her."

Aran gave his king a blatant 'don't be stupid' look. "Of course."

"Give me regular updates," Aranhil requested of the two of them. "I will manage things up here for you, Sellion. If you wish to write a quick letter to your business partner and Master, I will relay them for you."

That was infinitely kind of him and Sevana agreed immediately. "Please."

"Sellion," Lorien called to her from his chellomi, "I have writing materials."

Perfect. Sevana slogged the rest of the way to the shore, reaching up for the paper, pencil, and the small writing board that he had on him. Lorien was always the most prepared out of the group. She wrote hastily, her handwriting sloppier than usual, and forced herself several times to slow down before it became completely illegible. Her note to Morgan was quick and to the point. The one to Master was slightly more comprehensive, as he had a better grasp on the magical side of things. To both, she requested that they shut down her business for the next year, as it would take at least that long for her to figure out how to work magic once again.

If she ever could work as an Artifactor again. Sevana was not convinced she would be able to pick up the threads of her life after this.

The thought made her chest jitter in strange ways, but she forced the building anxiety aside, as it had no place in this moment. She didn't have much of a choice but to move forward. Time would tell how the chips would fall.

Finished, she folded both letters, wrote the recipient's name on the outside, and handed them to Lorien. "Thank you."

Leaning forward in the saddle, Lorien confided, "I will be relieved to give them good news. Good luck, Sellion. Know that if you need us, we'll come."

She smiled up at him without really thinking about it. "I know. Hopefully I'll see you before the seasons change." She paused, thought about sending a letter to the Sa Kao monarchy, explaining why the Fae had been pissed off enough to level a building…then thought better of it. The researchers—if anyone had survived—could do their own explaining. And it wasn't something that a letter could cover. When she had a chance to sit down, she'd contact Milly by mirror and see if she couldn't somehow rig a two-way call via the mirrors to properly sort that out. Maybe a three-way, as Aranhil should definitely be involved as well.

Sevana returned to the water's edge, not surprised when Aran stayed right next to her, practically hovering. He'd probably be like this for days until his panic receded. Sevana would try not to kill him in the meantime. She almost told Ursilla they could go back down but thought better of it. "Aranhil. Don't think this means you can empty Big and shut everything down. I'm not immediately moving into South Woods after this."

Patting her on the head like a child, Aranhil smiled. "We'll talk about it later."

That had not been a yes. Sevana glared at him. "I mean it. If I have to put everything back in place, I will be quite cross with you."

"We won't touch anything yet," he soothed her, still in that patronizing tone of voice.

She did not trust him. At all. Giving him a warning look, she decided to send another message to Master or Sarsen, get someone to check in regularly with Big. "Alright, Ursilla, I suppose we're ready."

"Then let us go down."

With a negligent flick of the fingers, Ursilla created an air bubble around them, drawing them down into the cold and dark world of the sea. Sevana forced herself to breathe, as she instinctively wanted to hold her breath. She always did for some reason. It was and wasn't like having a glass bowl shaped around them as they descended into the sea, a stationary thing that moved with them. The difference, of course, being that it wasn't solid like glass and she could put her hand straight through it if she chose to. Sometimes schools of dish darted in close, but they automatically veered away from the three people walking along the wet ocean floor, avoiding a collision. Only when several feet of water rose above their heads as they descended did she think to ask the obvious question. "Aran, you have no luggage, do you?"

"Nor do you," he observed with an unconcerned shrug. "We chose to move light and fast, I had no time to think of packing. Your things are still on your ship. Don't worry, someone stayed behind to arrange shipping it back. I'm the only one who knows how to pilot it, after all."

Yes, that was true, hence Sevana's brief flare of panic. She had a terrible mental vision of someone trying their hand at flying and crashing the ship into Nopper's Woods. "Right. Good. Well, I suppose we'll just have to depend on Rane and Curano's hospitality. Nothing we own is suitable for underwater living anyway. Its colder down here and we'll inevitably get wet at some point. Their clothes are better suited for this environment."

"True enough." Aran's fingers reached out, tangling lightly with hers, just the tips brushing. "You're alright with this?"

Sevana nearly gave him a blithe assurance, but they had been through too much with each other for her to just dismiss his concerns. "I'm not sure. But I feel like it's the only path forward. I can't stay as I am. I can't have my body reset to what it was. This is the only thing I can do."

He nodded, his hold on her hand tightening. "You won't be alone through this."

Snorting a laugh, Sevana drawled, "Of all the things I'm worried about, that wasn't one of them."

Aran shared her grin for a moment, eyes soft and warm with affection. "Yes, I suppose I am a guaranteed thing, aren't I?"

"It's good you're aware of that." Shaking her head, she let out a low breath. Even though she'd known that Aran would be with her through all of this, somehow she'd needed to hear that reassurance. "Just so you know, Rane's got a problem down here that she wants me to solve after my magic's straightened out. They've got some sort of transportation device that's not working correctly."

He cocked his head slightly. "The cost of giving you the help you need?"

"It was never said, only implied. But yes, I think that's exactly what it is." Sevana shrugged, as it didn't bother her. In fact, it might be a blessing in disguise. Best for her to have a magical problem to solve while she whiled the weeks away, waiting for her transformation to reach completion. And it would be good to see if she really could solve magical problems once her magic was wholly restored to her again.

Ursilla tilted her head just enough to say over her shoulder, "It is a rather complex system, in fact. It connects our nation with the other Unda nations, and even leads to some openings in the sea caves to allow us access to land. It has not worked properly in the past two decades, and our own engineers have not been able to determine why. The system only works intermittently."

That was far more informative than what Rane had said in passing. Interesting. Sevana had no real working knowledge of Unda magic and was intrigued by the project. Would this be a dichotomy of magic, something opposite of how Fae magic worked? Similar?

Sevana assumed the latter; after all, the Unda and Fae were cousins, so their blood worked along similar lines. But nothing she had seen so far had been akin to Fae construction, which made her wonder.

Aran snorted a laugh, his eyes warm on her. "I swear, you're only happy when you have a puzzle to solve."

"Be grateful I have a puzzle to solve," Sevana retorted without heat. "Otherwise I'll be languishing down here like some damsel in distress and climbing the walls in boredom."

He blanched at the idea. "Ye merciful gods, preserve us from that."

She laughed, because Aran of all people understood just how well she dealt with boredom—which was to say, not at all. He'd been one of the few people brave enough to stay with her during her convalescence, and he had not come out of that time completely unscathed. "You see? Rane's actually doing me more of a favor than she realizes."

Aran nodded in fervent agreement. "I'll extend my heartfelt thanks when I see her. Ursilla, you said before that you must have my blood to help you. Is there any other aid that I can render?"

The ancient Unda shook her head gently. "This is not a process that anyone else can put their hand upon. It is not wise to have too many influences during this. Simply lend your blood and attention when I call for it."

"And keep me out of trouble," Sevana tacked on with a maniacal grin. "You'll have your hands full just doing that."

Giving a long sigh, Aran muttered under his breath, "That is the most profound understatement ever uttered under the sea."

Sevana cackled again, not denying it. If she had to be stuck under the ocean for weeks—possibly months—at a stretch, then at least she had someone with her to torment and tease.

3

Rane either moved very quickly or she'd been plotting for a while on how to keep Sevana down under the sea. Sevana darkly suspected the latter. Rane was nothing if not determined and sneaky. Sevana wasn't inclined to complain, considering the lateness of the hour. It was nearing midnight at this point, and despite her enforced nap earlier, she wanted nothing more than a horizontal perch and quiet.

Her underwater home for the next few weeks was at least inviting. The outer shell of it had been formed with coral reefs that overlapped each other, growing in a multiple menagerie of hues and species, yet somehow avoiding a slapdash appearance. It was quite obviously grown and cultivated to look this particular way, to form this particular dome shape. The inside of it glowed, as if crushed florescent rock had been applied to the ceilings and walls. A strongly applied elemental magic layered all throughout the top, stretching out along most of the street so that Sevana could walk and breathe without attempting to grow gills in the next fifteen seconds. The floor was firmer here, a polished stone that looked like andesite to her eyes, which made sense, as the ocean floor was largely made of sediment and volcanic rock. True bed linens and furniture sat artfully arranged, appearing as if they'd just walked off some landbound furniture store. Sevana had stayed in worse places, no question.

Of course, her guest house was nestled into a neighborhood of similar looking houses, all of them of the same general build and construction materials. They looked so much alike that she'd have trouble finding this one again easily. Some of the houses had planters outside of their doors—collections of flower-like anemones with their delicate white feathery edges, or bold red centers, like peonies—or strategically grown coral reefs in their shades of purples. The planter boxes didn't just liven up the place in between the dark grey sea rocks of the streets, but also would serve as landmarks. And Sevana would need the landmarks.

Still, as inviting as this large, domed cottage under the sea appeared, it grated that she had to be here, so far from the comforts of home. Or perhaps it was the uneasy anticipation of what the next few weeks would entail that made Sevana's nerves cringe. Ursilla had promised that Sevana's body and magic could be changed over to Fae.

She never promised it would be painless.

Sevana moved further inside, investigating and taking in her surroundings, trying to prod her tired mind into making a list of possible needs for the upcoming weeks. Sadly, she could only anticipate the next twenty-four hours and gave up the attempt. She'd think in the morning.

Stopping in the middle of her new room, she looked back around carefully. The cottage basically seemed to be split up into four rooms. A main room, which she stood in, that held a low couch and a stack of cushions; a kitchenette area with a sink, counter, and a table to eat at; a bathing room tucked off to the side of the kitchen, and a bedroom that had nothing more than a bed and a rug on the floor. Sparse furnishing, certainly, but the place wasn't big enough to hold much in the way of furniture. Turning to her guide, a young Unda by the name of Khan, she gave him a nod. "This is fine."

"It is not," Aran immediately denied, staring about the room with his brows twisted together in consideration. "Bring another bed in here. The main room is fine." As if anticipating her protest, Aran moved a step in closer, his eyes intense, voice low but penetrating. "We have no idea how the change will affect you. I'm not leaving your side until it's finished."

It was on the tip of her tongue to rejoin that she didn't need a babysitter, that he could find his own guest house to stay in. Those words almost flew out of her mouth in sheer instinct, but something stopped her from saying it. Perhaps the look on Aran's face, his expression saying that he expected an argument on this. Perhaps the look on Ursilla's as she watched them, knowing but with a grim line around her eyes.

The easy transition that a child went through from human to Fae was incremental, an almost natural evolution done in daily doses so that as the child grew, they changed with nothing more than normal growing pains. What Sevana would embark on in the next two months would be anything but gradual, and she was only the third in known history to undergo it. The first magician to do so. No one, including Ursilla, knew exactly how her body and magic would react to this.

As much as having someone watch over her grated upon her pride, Sevana had to admit that out of everyone in her inner circle, if she had to choose someone, Aran would be her first choice. He was patient enough to not kill her when she started climbing the walls, and she liked him enough to not attempt murder when her frustration levels hit their peak.

She couldn't manage to say anything mushy or sentimental. The words tangled in her brain before ever reaching her mouth. What came out instead was, "Just don't hover."

Aran lit up in a relieved smile. "Promise I won't."

"Chance would be a fine thing," Sevana groused to no one in particular. "Khan, get another bed and chair in here. Clothes for both of us, too. And if you can lay your hands on land food, that would be best. We're not fond of raw fish."

Khan looked actually relieved at these clear instructions—Sevana suspected she was the first human he'd ever actually been this close to—and ducked his head in a quick bow. "I will see to it myself, Artifactor." He gave her another bow before scampering off.

Come to think of it, was he to be their host while staying here? Sevana had only been here overnight once, but she'd had a hostess who cooked and cleaned and basically served as a housekeeper during her stay. Sevana hadn't thought of Khan as their host, he seemed a little young for the role, but apparently he was.

With him dispatched, Sevana turned her attention to Ursilla. "Alright. What are we actually doing?"

"It is too late to start things tonight, and we are all fatigued from a harried experience," Ursilla announced, stopping at the door. "Now that I know where you are staying, I will find my own bed. I will come again in the morning to start your treatments."

It was the sensible approach and Sevana nodded, grateful she didn't have to tackle anything else today. "Yes, alright."

"Good night," Aran offered her.

With a polite inclination of the head, Ursilla moved off, elegant with every stride.

Tugging off her boots, Sevana flopped onto the bed, bouncing once before settling with her eyes closed and arms outspread. Still, even as fatigue dragged at her, certain questions boiled to the surface. "How did you find me?"

"Milly helped. She went looking for your mirror on board, and was able to give me a clue on where you'd been taken. Between her efforts and Tashjian, we figured out where you were and that you'd been kidnapped. Again." Aran's weight settled next to her on the bed, one leg tucked up under the other. He sounded wrecked, the strain and fatigue of the day taking their toll. "We need to locate a mirror and assure her you're alright. I'll take care of that in a minute."

Sevana made a vague gesture with one hand. "I'll do it."

"It would require you getting up," Aran pointed out sardonically.

She immediately reconsidered. "You can do it."

Snorting, he muttered, "I thought so. How are you, Sevana?"

"Tired, irritated, but not hurt," she assured him, making the supreme effort to open her eyes and roll her head enough to look up at him. The worry lines around his eyes and mouth aged him a decade, which was saying something, as the Fae had to be very, very old before they wore their years on their skin. "They didn't actually do anything to me, aside from the kidnapping and illegal potion dosing. I apparently was messing with the magic of the world, creating magical eddies that clashed and upset the balance, hence my kidnapping."

"If you're trying to make me feel guilty about the Institute being torn to shreds, you can save your breath," he retorted, a bite of fire in the words.

Yes, that was clearly a lost cause. "I was mostly trying to reassure you."

"Ah." He blinked and his anger faded a notch, leaving him tired and agreeable on the surface once more. "I'm glad, then. I assure you everyone else is fine. I stopped in at Big while waiting for you to come home, and no one showed up there."

"I'm not surprised. It was me they were after." She paused as a knock sounded on the outer door. "I think your bed is here."

"Yes, apparently so." Aran went up to oversee its placement.

Sevana rolled over, intending to get up and see things as well, but only made it to her side before a new wave of exhaustion hit her. That sedative potion had not, apparently, completely cleared her system. She recognized the signs well enough. Well, it didn't matter, Aran could handle his own bed.

The thought had barely finished before she was firmly in dreamland.

Khan made sure they had new clothes and breakfast waiting by the time they arose the next morning. Sevana barely had clothes on and a full belly when Ursilla came knocking, proving the woman to be an early riser. Or she was like most elderly people and didn't sleep much.

"Good morning," Aran greeted, waving her inside before shutting the door behind her.

"Good morning," she returned, although her eyes scanned Sevana from head to toe and back again. "You seem more alert this morning. Good. Are you ready to begin?"

Seeing no reason to delay it, Sevana settled for a confirming nod and dropped into one of the chairs. "Tell me what we'll be doing."

Ursilla moved to sit on one of the chairs, crammed though it was with Aran's bed in the way. She got comfortable before answering. "Sit, both of you, this will take a few moments to explain. Sellion, you are likely well aware that your magic will not take to changes kindly."

Snorting, Sevana gave her a grim nod. "I know that painfully well."

Inclining her head, Ursilla matched her grim expression. "Then you know this will not be easy; there is no way of knowing exactly how your body will react throughout the metamorphosis. I have a notion that if we try to shut off your magic first, that might aid us in the long run. But I think I'm getting ahead of myself. What we will do is take each fuinnimh and apply Arandur's blood directly to it."

Sevana threw up a hand. "My what?"

"Fuinnimh," Aran translated, settling cross-legged on the floor, reclining his back against her shins. "Think of them like the energy points along the body."

"Ah, like chakra points," Sevana said in understanding. "Alright, I think I understand. Go on, Ursilla."

Ursilla had an odd look upon her face, her eyes darting between Aran and Sevana, as if he had just done something strange, and Ursilla was dying to ask why. She was slow to pick the explanation back up. "In fact, I will not be directly changing you. Arandur will be, under my guidance. I will ride herd upon the change so that his blood does not react in your body like an unruly seahorse. I estimate that if your body can withstand the changes, we might be able to turn you fully Fae within six weeks. Three months at most."

That six weeks sounded like a better time frame. Sevana drew in a breath, trying to adjust to the idea that in six weeks, she would be full-fledged Fae. Of all the things that she'd expected to happen in her life, never had this been one of them. Even with Aranhil threatening to turn her fully Fae over the past several months, she hadn't really considered this to be the path her life would take. No one had thought it really feasible, even though they kept discussing it as an option.

The enormity of the decision she'd made started to crash down upon her like ocean waves. Her life would never be the same after this. Living in Big, going about in the human world, that would slowly change. Her life would be ever more caught up in South Woods as her human connections slowly disappeared one by one. The thought left her unmoored in a disturbing way, as if she were in danger of drifting off in a helter-skelter manner. No, she could worry about all of that later. It was the transition that she should focus on now, and that was disturbing enough.

Warm hands gripped hers, hard, and she snapped back into the present to see Aran's cool green eyes looking up at her in worry. She squeezed back, thankful beyond reckoning that he was so steadfast in his support of her. Sevana hadn't wanted to admit it, but she really did need a friend during all of this. Even with him at her side, this was frightening enough. Doing it alone would have been frankly terrifying.

"We don't have to start this today," he assured her gently. "We don't have to do a thing until you're ready."

Shaking her head, Sevana drew in a shaky breath, trying to settle her nerves. She felt strangely nauseous and pushed that down, too. "We've already given this a lot of time. I'm just irrationally panicking, pay me no mind. Ursilla, if we're doing my magic first, then I assume the first change will be near my heart?"

"Yes." Ursilla watched her with open concern as well. "Are you sure, child? He's right, we don't have to start until you're ready."

"I'm just nervous," Sevana assured them both, trying to mean it. "But sitting on this longer won't help with that. I'll feel better once I'm committed and working towards a goal. It's alright. How does Aran start the change? Tell me I don't have to drink blood like a vampire."

Ursilla and Aran both snorted in amusement and shared wry glances. "Nothing like that," Ursilla assured her. "Arandur will prick his finger and draw a specific symbol on your skin. We'll carefully manage how much blood he uses—it won't be more than a few drops—and precisely where he'll put them. Arandur, you are familiar with the symbols, I trust, as you started her change to begin with."

"I know the basic three," he answered with a shrug.

"Ah. In that case, I must teach you the more advanced symbol, as this will take high magick." Ursilla glided up and over to a nearby side table, rustling about until she found a pot of squid ink, quill, and paper. Coming back to him, she sketched out a very complicated looking knot before handing it over. "Do this ten times."

Aran accepted the writing materials from her and dutifully leaned over on the floor to carefully practice drawing it out.

Leaning over his shoulder, Sevana studied it for a moment. She'd not seen this particular knotwork before, but she'd seen plenty similar. To this day, no one quite knew how the humans discovered the elements and symbols that the Fae used in their complex magicks, just that they had. They were quite taken with the beauty and intricacy of the designs and often copied them into their art, the decorative trim on their houses, and most often their jewelry. It amused Sevana sometimes when she saw it, as now she knew what most of those symbols did, and seeing the dichotomy of those symbols on people cracked her up often. She'd once seen a young mother wandering about with an infertility necklace on, which Sevana found incredibly ironic.

Ursilla stopped Aran on the fifth practice symbol. "I think you have it. That's perfect."

"One more," he requested, still bent over the page. "I want to make sure I'm comfortable with this."

Sevana, focused on practical matters, looked down at her shirt. She was in her typical white shirt, a warm coat, and pants as Khan had matched her style while shopping for her. The laced-up collar could possibly be pulled aside and down enough for Aran to have the room he needed to draw in, but she'd have to ditch the coat first. Decided, she unbuttoned it and shrugged her way out before hanging it on the back of the chair.

Grunting in satisfaction, Aran sat up on his heels. "Alright, I think I'm ready. Ursilla, how much blood precisely?"

"Three drops, if you can manage it. No more than five."

Nodding at these directions, he slipped a dagger free from the sheath at his waist and carefully pricked his index finger. As he moved, so did Sevana, pulling her shirt down and parting it in the middle. He looked up, all business-like, took one look at her partially exposed chest, and froze, blood rushing up into his face.

"Aran." Sevana regarded him with frank amusement. Look at that blush. She'd never seen him beet red before; it was bad enough she nearly offered him a cooling charm. "I'm still perfectly decent. It's not like I'm flashing my breasts at you. What are you blushing about?"

Clearing his throat, he pointedly did not answer that question. Gulping, he carefully placed his finger right above her heart and gently drew the symbol on in a red smear of blood. Sevana watched him do so in open interest, her senses allowing her to see not only physically how he moved, but magically the impact it had on her. The Fae blood absorbed into her skin almost on contact, where it directly countered the human magic flowing sluggishly in her core, mixing in like oil with water, rising to the top and then slowly filtering down in a way that spoke of suppression.

She watched it avidly, morbidly curious on how her magic would react next. The first twitch along her core felt more like a flinch of protest rather than actual pain. The second had more of an 'ouch' sting to it, the Fae blood directly suppressing her magic. Sevana watched in growing alarm as the blood not only tried to suppress her magic core, but started invading it outright, skewering right through it.

White-hot pain shattered through her chest, writhing as if she'd been poked a hundred times with hot red pokers. A scream strangled in the back of her throat as she doubled over, head gone fuzzy and white with nothing but sensation, her rational mind overwhelmed.

"Sevana?!" Aran's hands were on her shoulders, voice climbing high in panic.

"Don't get any more blood on her!" Ursilla commanded sharply. "Remove that hand. Move, let me see her."

Different hands touched her next, cool hands that smelled of the sea, but Sevana couldn't bring her head up enough to check. Her body shuddered, jerking as if she were seized by an illness, and Sevana certainly felt like she'd been hit by a plague, magical attack, and some torture chamber rack at the same time. Her nerves were alight with sparking, arcing energy that felt like it would either light her on fire or tear her apart at any moment. It took all of her focus just to breathe.

Something happened, some force bent itself upon her, something cold that felt blissful against her overheated body. It didn't stop the battle waging inside of her magical core, but it did lessen the impact, and Sevana drew her first full breath, spots dancing in front of her eyes.

"That's better," Aran said in frank relief, hovering off somewhere to the side. "Great spirits, I thought she was going to tear herself apart for a moment there."

"Felt like it, too," Sevana gasped out against her knees. She thought about sitting up, but the twinges in her chest still sparked like angry will o' wisps, and staying in this half-fetal position sounded like a better option for the next while. "Ursilla, how is it?"

"This is not quite what I imagined. Because your magical power is lower than most magicians, I didn't think we'd have much of a battle on our hands." Ursilla's hands moved in deliberate patterns along her back, the sweep of her hands calming the tumultuous upheaval happening internally. "I'll have to keep a close eye on you tonight, I think. You won't pass the next day easily, but rest easy, child. You'll survive the change."

Sevana was delighted to hear it. For a moment there, she hadn't shared that confidence. "At least the worst part is over, right?"

A noncommittal hum answered her. That sound spoke volumes.

"You could at least lie and make me feel better," Sevana grumbled irately.

At that, Ursilla cackled lowly. "You'll live, child."

That wasn't in the least bit comforting.

Knowing that the letter would take a while to reach anyone, Sevana did the sensible thing. She had her little host, Khan, fetch a mirror for her, then she propped it up in the main room on the table and called for Milly.

Milly must have been hovering in this general direction of the world, as she heard her much faster than Sevana expected her to. The spirit of the mirror popped up into the oval-shaped frame like a ghost, suddenly and without any warning. "Sevana! Great stonking deities, but you gave me a fright."

"Gave everyone a fright, but I maintain that it was not my fault," Sevana responded, not at all bothered by the scolding tone. She sat cross-legged in the chair at a very careful angle to keep her aching body from clamoring. Sevana could tell the blood treatment was working, as she felt little aftershocks rock through her nervous system at random. It made for uncomfortable times. Aran was in the next bedroom, trying on clothes to see what Khan had bought him that would fit. He was a smidge taller than most of the Unda, so that made it interesting. "They got the drop on me. And I was under a sedative spell when the Unda snatched me back."

Shaking her head, the matron gave her a sympathetic look. "You have had a whirlwind month, haven't you? So where are you now?"

Sevana filled her in, giving her the broad picture of where she was and what they were planning to do next. "I've got letters heading to Master and Kip, but do me a favor and drop in to both of them, spread the word, then drop in and tell Bel the same. I don't want him sending for me only to get a nasty surprise. He's a little too quick to race off to the rescue sometimes."

"I'll do so," Milly promised faithfully. "But what about you? How are you taking this?"

That was indeed the question. "I'm…alright with it. Well, really, I don't see any other way of living life without being constantly hobbled by my own magic. And I can't live like that."

Milly nodded, but she had her bottom lip clutched between her teeth, expression doubtful. "Will it really be better?"

"My alternative is a short life span with semi-volatile magic. What do you think?"

"Well, I agree it doesn't sound good, but…" her voice dropped to a more confidential whisper. "I know Tashjian worries about you becoming fully Fae."

"Yes, well, so do I. But the only thing that really worries me about it is staying permanently in South Woods. You know I'd go crazy if I tried to keep myself locked into one location. If I just knew that I could work as an Artifactor even with Fae magic…" Sevana trailed off, thinking hard. It sounded incredulous on the surface, being both at once, but really, she couldn't think of a reason why she couldn't. Except that no one had done it before. And when had that ever stopped her?

Milly must have been thinking along the same lines, as her expression echoed Sevana's own thoughts. "Is there something to stop you from doing the same work?"

"I don't know," Sevana admitted sourly. She really hated those words. "I think it'll take some thought and a little research on my part to figure it out. But right now, I still see it is a possibility. I'm just not sure how viable it is."

"I trust you to figure it out." Milly gave a glance over her shoulder. "I think someone's trying to call me. Likely wondering if I've heard from you."

"Go see who it is," Sevana encouraged, "but before you go, one more favor. Ask Master if he can figure out how to tie this mirror in with a few others. I need to hold a conference of sorts with Aranhil and the Sa Kao king. My Fae family destroyed the Cope Research Institute—"

Milly muttered something that sounded like 'don't blame them.'

"—and if that isn't smoothed over then it's going to put bad blood in the water. I'd rather not come home to high tensions, thank you very much." She winced, not only at the mental image her words conjured, but at another spike of pressure rocking through her system. Hissing a soft breath between clenched teeth, she waited for the sensation to fade.

The cant of her head and purse of her lips said Milly understood her stance, but Sevana sensed that her friend still sided with the Fae on this one. "I'll pass it along. Anything else?"

"No, not right now. I'm sure Master will have a shopping list for me, since I'm down here anyway. I'll fetch things for him and Sarsen, in return for their help at Big. But tell them not to be too outlandish; I'll likely be on my sickbed for most of this." As if reminded, her magical core gave a painful twinge. Sevana put a hand over the area, rubbing a soothing circle.

Catching the gesture, Milly asked softly, "Does it hurt?"

"It's not pleasant." Sighing, she shook her head. "It's fine, I'll survive. Off with you. Let me know what's happening back home."

"Be safe," Milly instructed, nearly scolded, then she disappeared again, leaving the mirror as a blank surface once more.

Sevana stared at her own reflection for a moment and finally understood why everyone kept asking if she were alright. She really didn't look it. Her skin was too tight over her bones, bruises under her eyes, and even to her, her magic looked sick. Like she had leprosy in her magical core. It was a wonder they hadn't insisted on putting her in some sort of hospital, really.

The next six weeks would be tedious, painful, and exhausting. She did not at all look forward to it, but hopefully the end result would be worth it.

4

Arandur spent the rest of the night sitting next to Sevana's bed. She'd not had an easy day of it, her side effects progressively getting worse, and while she'd been vocal enough about her discomfort, she hadn't actually complained much. He could see intimately well just what her body was going through, the torques against her magical core, and knew it couldn't be painless. She hissed in a painful breath now and again, turning and trying different positions for a more comfortable posture, but to no avail. He soothed her as he could, bringing in wet clothes and cold stones to help mitigate her fevers that came and went. Every effort felt borderline useless, but she didn't seem to think so. Every time the pain became too intense for her to manage, she reached out for him, latching onto his hands or arms in a vice that left bruises.

The worst of it, thankfully, seemed to have passed. Arandur knew it to be sometime early in the morning, perhaps a few hours from sunrise, and Sevana had finally found some respite. She lay on her side in the bed, a thin blanket draped over her, the lights dim to encourage sleep. Even in this cold sea, she still felt hot to the touch, and though they had a heavier comforter at hand, Arandur left it folded at the foot of the bed. Sweat beaded along her forehead already; she didn't need another covering.

He sat on the floor, his arms folded and resting on the mattress, keeping watch over her. Arandur knew he should rest but could not make himself actually get to his feet and find his own bed. He'd been through too many scares where Sevana was concerned in the past month and right now, seeing her, knowing that he could reach past the six inches that separated them and touch her, did his heart the most good.

Of course, if she woke up at this moment, she'd tartly inform him that spying upon sleeping women was creepy and to quit it. The thought made him smile, briefly. He'd take the teasing right now over this pain-racked woman who could barely string a full sentence together. Rain and stars, he couldn't wait for this transformation to be over.

To this day, he felt conflicted about what he'd done. Putting his blood in her had been the only way to save Sevana's life. Even now, months later, Arandur couldn't think of another method that would have worked. As much trouble as it had caused—and stars knew it'd caused quite a bit—Sevana had never once told him that he'd made a mistake. She appreciated being alive, even though her body and magic gave her so much trouble. Arandur was glad for that, because even if she'd grown vexed with him for his choice, he couldn't bring himself to regret it.

Still, he wasn't blind to her struggles, either. The magic was one thing, but Sevana worried how becoming Fae in the future would impact her life. Part of the reason why they always took a human child to change was because it made the transition easier. The child didn't have to worry about careers, households, adult obligations to fulfill. Children were still growing and finding their place in the world anyway, so of course the progression was natural. Sevana would now have to make all those decisions and find a way to compromise between her human self and her new status as Fae.

Aranhil likely would not make it easy on her, either. He was quite delighted to finally have her fully within his realm. Arandur and the Mothers had cautioned their king several times to take it easy, to draw Sellion gradually into her rightful place of South Woods, but Aranhil was so enthusiastic about it that he likely wouldn't have much patience.

Considering Sevana's own level of patience, it was just a matter of time before they butted heads. Arandur's money was not on his king.

"You need to sleep."

Arandur's eyes snapped up, vaguely surprised to see Sevana looking back at him. Her eyes were mere slits, voice a husky shell compared to its normal timbre, but her attention was sharp and focused compared to what it had been. "Did I wake you?"

She gave the most minute shake of the head. "Thirsty."

"Hold on." He rolled up to his knees, feeling his joints creak a little at the sudden movement after hours of holding the same position. The carafe and glasses sitting nearby were not ice cold, but the warm temperature of the water would actually feel better to her overheated system right now anyway. He poured a full glass before coming back to her, slipping an arm under her torso to lift her half-up, making it easier to drink.

Sevana had one hand over his on the glass to help anchor herself and she gulped the water down noisily. With a sigh, she pushed it back when most of it was gone and leaned her head against his shoulder, letting him support most of her weight. "Sarsen poisoned me with a bad batch of mushroom soup once."

Amused, he tilted his head so that he could see her expression. "Is that comparable to now?"

"No, but I'll tell him it was."

Snorting, he set the glass aside. "You must be feeling better if you're already planning on how to torment someone. You still feel hot to me."

"Starting to feel cold," she admitted, snuggling further into him. "You're warm."

Arandur did not mind having a lapful of Sevana, and he adjusted her so they were both comfortable, then snagged her blanket to drape over her. A hand against her forehead still felt damp with sweat, but cooler than it had been an hour ago, suggesting the fever was breaking. A good sign. However, Sevana was not a snuggler, and if she were actively seeking him out, it suggested that she was feeling worse than she'd let on. Arandur gladly gave her the tactile comfort of touch, soothing her as he could, but this out-of-character behavior worried him.

"Why did Ursilla react like that this morning?" Sevana's voice lilted up in curiosity, her words brushing like warm air against his throat. "She kept staring, after you sat down near my feet."

It took him a moment to realize what she referred to. "Ah, that? The Fae show dominance or position by height." Arandur shrugged, as if this wasn't anything earth-shattering or momentous. "By sitting as I did, I showed that you are higher in status than I am."

Sevana pulled back to stare at him in growing perplexity. "Since when do I have a higher status than you? I'm half-Fae, an adopted member; how could I possibly be higher than you?"

For some reason this question amused him, and his eyebrows arched up as he answered, half-teasing. "You're a magical expert, not to mention the person who has brought us multiple children. I'm just a tracker."

"Arandur." Sevana's tone was firm, brooking no disagreement. "You are not *just* anything."

A feeling of heat rose and turned his face hot. Trying to subdue the blush, he teased back, "I'm glad you think so."

"Fine, don't believe me," she grumbled, snuggling back in. "Although I have to tell you, if anyone else tried to hover and be cuddly with me, I would have handed them their own head by now. You're at least sympathetic without being clingy."

"High praise," he allowed softly, filled to bursting with the need to turn his head just so and kiss her forehead. It was hard, but he checked himself. He didn't have the right to those liberties yet. He may not ever earn it. But that was a problem for a different day. Today, Sevana took priority.

She fell asleep again, breath soft and steady, body entirely lax in his arms. Loathe to move and risk waking her, Arandur instead stayed as he was, relaxing against the bed frame and waiting for the rest of the world to wake up. No doubt his hosts would have some choice words to say about him overstepping his bounds and being so familiar with his superior, but Sevana had already made her wishes clear, and

Arandur had no intention of listening to anyone else but her.

Ursilla came to check on Sevana just before breakfast. The tight expression on her face voiced her displeasure at finding Sevana half-curled into Aran's lap, but she didn't say anything. Or, more accurately, she chose to wait until Sevana was in the bathing room washing off the sweat and changing into fresh clothes before voicing her opinion. Sevana could clearly hear her voice through the closed door.

"Arandur of South Woods. Your behavior is not appropriate."

"My behavior is whatever it needs to be in order to safeguard Sevana and ease her through this transition," he retorted heatedly, although he kept his voice down to avoid anyone else overhearing this argument.

Sevana snorted to herself. Yes, that was exactly how she expected Aran to respond to that. He had no patience with society's formalities. She didn't either. That's why they got along so well. It took no effort for her to listen even as she splashed water on her face, so she unabashedly eavesdropped. Although oww, leaning at this angle over the bowl was tugging painfully on her lower back.

Not happy with his response, the elder Unda responded in a growl, like a leviathan upon waking crankily from a bad nap. "You would be wise to remember your place."

"My place is wherever she is," he riposted sharply. "Do not mistake *your* position in this, Unda. I am her companion, one tasked with the duty to safeguard her until she is whole again, and I will do whatever it is she asks of me. If Sevana finds my behavior inappropriate, she will tell me so. She's not shy about that sort of thing."

Really, what was Ursilla's problem? Offering comfort to a friend in the dead of night was still comfort, no matter the mixed genders. Fed up with this scolding, Sevana yanked her shirt on—which oww, she shouldn't have done that, either—before she grabbed the door and pulled it sharply open, revealing her damp and scowling self framed in the doorway. "No, I am not. Ursilla, I'm aware that technically

I outrank him, and there's some hierarchy that says he's not on the same level I'm on. It's stupid, all of it. I wouldn't be alive without Aran. He's saved me more times than I can count. You're not going to get on your high horse and tell him that giving me the comfort and help I asked for last night was 'inappropriate.'"

Ursilla's thin brows arched, not in surprise, but in challenge. "You are young. You do not understand our ways yet."

Crossing her arms over her chest, Sevana glared back at her. "I've argued with kings, lady. They didn't win. You don't stand much of a better chance than they did. You don't get to tell my friend what he can and cannot do around me."

A battle of wills commenced, both women locking glares, neither willing to back down. The air practically crackled with energy and Aran looked ready to listen to his survival instincts and make a run for it. Sevana didn't have control of her magic right now, but he wouldn't put it past her to toss around explosive spells if a fight got thrown her direction. She knew exactly what he was thinking.

The tension built to nearly lethal levels. Aran started looking for the best path to the door. Then, strangely, Ursilla smiled, the expression shark-like in her pale skin. "Stars, but you have guts, child. I now understand why Nia Reign likes you and trusted you as her Voice. You are fully as blood-thirsty as she is."

"Darn straight I am," Sevana muttered, mostly to herself. Chin lifted, she faced Ursilla down. "My Aran. Don't fuss on him."

Aran beamed at her in pure delight. Which did funny things to Sevana's heart strings. For some reason, seeing that expression on his face, Sevana wanted to do something else to make him smile. Why was that?

Lifting her hands in surrender, Ursilla promised, "I will not interfere again. Are you ready for the next step?"

Sighing gustily, Sevana put the strange thought aside and focused on Ursilla again. While she felt like something Baby dragged in, she was improved over last night, and delaying things wouldn't help at this stage just because she felt like death warmed over. "Might as well. Another against my magical core?"

"I do believe another is necessary, but not today. I fear overloading your body will only put you into shock. Let us avoid heart failure," Ursilla responded in a casual tone that did not match the terrifying words she uttered.

Sevana felt terrified at the picture she painted. Could they really have overloaded her heart by just charging blindly ahead? Wait, did the Fae in the room understand that the human body was frailer than that of the Fae's? Hopefully they did. Sevana would be in a world of trouble otherwise.

Trying not to let on how unnerved she was by that casual statement, she inquired, "So what next, then?"

"I think your senses," Ursilla suggested, tapping a thoughtful finger to her chin. "They take the longest to adjust, and having them properly aligned will help you recover your magical control later. Arandur, we need to place that same symbol against her forehead."

That sounded infinitely better to her, far less risky. Not to mention probably more comfortable. Her magical core still felt like someone had stabbed a knitting needle into it. Giving that a few days to settle while working on the rest of her body seemed a sound plan.

Aran apparently agreed, as he slipped his dagger free from his waist sheath and once again pricked his index finger before carefully applying the blood to Sevana's forehead. The skin was slightly moist from her washing, making the blood smear on easier. Perhaps they should dampen her skin from now on before drawing upon it.

Sevana barely blinked as he drew, then stood waiting patiently as the blood seeped into her skin and started its changes. They all waited for the extreme reaction that she'd experienced the day before.

Several moments passed and she just stood there, looking idly around. Unlike last time, the blood didn't have an immediate effect on her. She still felt it, idly worming its way through her skin, but it wasn't as sharply uncomfortable as the first treatment.

Aran, eyes glued to her, asked hopefully, "Alright?"

"Seems so?" she responded with a splay of her hand. "Nothing's hurting, at least, which is a vast improvement over yesterday. Ursilla, will this take longer to notice?"

"Perhaps so." Ursilla lifted her shoulders in an elegant shrug. "So far, you have not reacted as the other two adults I changed. I believe this alteration will not be painful, but do expect it to be confusing. Nothing about the transformation of an adult into a Fae is easy, after all."

"Confusing how?" Sevana demanded.

Ursilla gave another shrug. "We shall see."

"And for that matter," Sevana hadn't been able to follow up on this before, but she had all of the time in the world now, "these other two people that you changed. Tell me about them."

Ursilla took a seat on the chair, silently indicating that this would take a while. Sevana went for a chair as well (better sit before her senses took a strange turn), with Aran copying his behavior from the day before and sitting with his back resting against her legs. Sevana would have protested—he could sit on his bed—but she had a feeling he had deliberately done it to tweak Ursilla's nose. The constipated look on Ursilla's face, at least, indicated she didn't like his position whatsoever. For that reason alone, Sevana decided that she wouldn't utter a peep, even if her legs fell asleep.

"In both cases, they were human men that were loved by the Unda." Ursilla settled back, focusing on Sevana as she related the tale. "I was very young when I attempted it the first time. It was with my first husband, and we did not do such a rushed job as we're doing now, but something more gradual. It took me ten years to change him. I kept him with me for nearly three hundred years before a bad storm took him. The second change was for my niece's husband. She, too, fell in love with a human man and asked me to change him. I did so, not quite as gradually, as they were in a different clan and traveling was hard during those days. That time we took a year to do the change. It was harder for him, but he persevered through it. We unfortunately lost them both not a decade later. That was when the Kesly Isle volcanoes first started to erupt."

Sevana grimaced in sympathy. So this was eighty or so years ago. "Why, if this was so recent a change, isn't this knowledge more widespread?"

Ursilla shook her head, mouth in a flat line. "We did not share the information. For one thing, we do not wish to encourage this trend. If humans discovered that we can do this, they'll want the power and long life of the Unda and the Fae. That is not always wise. Those who seek power rarely use it wisely."

That…yeah, Sevana could agree whole-heartedly with that. She'd seen that very thing play out often. "But that's why Rane knew immediately that you could help me. Why didn't she mention this before?"

"She did not wish to until I agreed to help. Once she explained who you were, and the circumstances, I did not have any objections." Ursilla considered her thoughtfully. "And I see now, having met you, that you do not hunger for power. You are a wise choice."

Coming from this woman, Sevana would take those words as high praise.

"But what of the changes those two other men went through?" Aran had a notebook out, jotting down notes as Ursilla spoke. "What can we expect?"

"I can only use my past experiences as a base template," Ursilla warned him, although she looked approvingly on the notebook in his lap. Glad someone was finally writing all of this down? Or perhaps pleased that he was taking her words so seriously. "Her magic will make things different, if not outright difficult. But the previous two times, we learned to still do things gradually, as much as we could. Focusing on only one section of the body was not wise. Better to take turns, to spread it out, to let the body adjust more or less in balance with itself. We did see strange symptoms. The senses especially did not always respond well and were either hypervigilant or shut down entirely until the transformation was complete."

Sevana took note of that, although hopefully it wouldn't happen to her. "Was that the only strange symptom?"

"No, at one point my niece's husband experienced heart and liver failure." Ursilla paused, as if that hadn't made Sevana's heart and liver twinge in sympathetic response. "That's how we learned to not focus on just one part of the body. But he did survive without problems."

Sevana rubbed at the bridge of her nose. Great dark magic, but this wasn't going to be ideal, was it? "So if it took you a year last time, why do you think it can be done in six weeks this time?"

"I do not think it can be done. I think it *must* be done. Your magical core will fight us every step of the way, and you're partially turned already. If we don't complete the transformation quickly, then your magical core will likely erupt with conflicting energy."

Sevana stared at her, like a woman waiting for the punchline of a bad joke. "But you said it might take as long as three months?"

"Well." Ursilla calmly smoothed the braid laying over her shoulder. "There might be complications."

Complications. Riiiight.

5

The changes came on gradually, so gradually that Sevana didn't realize anything was off until she had half-consumed breakfast. She paused in eating some creamy soup made with clams to stare at the boots waiting for her next to the door. They were pretty, a dark royal purple that laced halfway up her shins, and clearly more to Rane's taste than Sevana's. She'd only worn them once so far and was contemplating going out again today to get her hands on the transportation problem. If her head and body weren't going to contort into a ball of pain today, she didn't want to just sit around like a wilting damsel in distress.

But the sight of the boots stopped her.

Aran, ever alert and observant, paused with a glass halfway to his mouth. "What's wrong?"

"Purple," Sevana said slowly, "tastes strange."

He blinked at her, trying to decipher that. "Come again?"

"Purple tastes strange," she repeated, more sure of it now. "Green tastes fuzzy, but cool. Black tastes sticky."

A pinched expression on his face, he carefully replaced the glass on the table. "Your senses are confusing themselves. Just taste and sight?"

"So far." Taking another look at the table, her head cocked. "I take it back. I can see scents. It's like…" a strange thought occurred to her and she paused. No. Surely not. But the idea hooked strongly into her brain and, experimenter that she was, Sevana had to prove it one way or another. She tentatively poked at the tendril wafting over the soup pot and then nearly choked. "So. Touching scents is also now a thing. Feels…light and fuzzy, like thin strands of cotton."

Rubbing at his forehead, Aran regarded her steadily. "You're making my brain hurt just listening to you."

'Confusing' just might be the biggest understatement to leave Ursilla's mouth yet. Sevana had heard of illnesses where the senses got mixed up and the mind got the signals crossed. But actually *tasting* colors or touching smells was so incredibly strange that she didn't know whether to be fascinated or disturbed. In the end, fascination won out. "Aran, I'm going out for a walk after this. This is too fascinating; I must experiment."

"Of course," he grumbled half to himself, "because if my senses were suddenly hijacked by their counterparts, the natural thing to do is explore. Not call Ursilla."

Prosaically, she added, "I want to take a look at the transportation system."

"You want to take a look at the transportation system while your senses are being dodgy and unhelpful," he repeated doubtfully.

Mock-sweetly, she returned, "Well, I can always stay here and let you entertain me as I slowly go stir crazy."

Wincing, Aran immediately caved. "By all means, let's go poke at the faulty transportation systems."

Sevana cackled. The last time she'd been cooped up for weeks inside of Big, no one had come through the experience with their sanity wholly intact. Aran and Master were the only ones who'd truly survived, and even Master swore that next time she was seriously hurt, he'd put her in a self-sustaining spell and let her sleep until she woke up, fully restored.

For some reason, Aran's patience with her outlasted everyone else's. He made no secret that he was very fond of her, and Sevana would be flattered by that if she didn't suspect his survival instincts were faulty. Perhaps he was dropped on his head frequently as a child? Something had to explain it.

They finished breakfast, put on boots, and Sevana moved carefully, accommodating the lingering aches in her muscles and the tension in her lower back as she headed outside of the door. Hopefully moving about would loosen things up as her muscles warmed. The Unda town lay out like a vast labyrinth of interconnected sea caves, coral walls and buildings, and carved stone rising from the ocean floor like a graceful wave suspended in the water. Specific routes were protected by large walkways, air bubbles that stayed permanently fixated for anyone who chose to walk about on two legs and their landlubber guests. If she chose to leave this area, Sevana would have to tap into an Unda to create an air bubble for them and act as tour guide, which would happen eventually. Still, she'd been given directions to the main transportation engine and it wasn't far, perhaps three streets over, and mostly under the air dome, so for now at least she didn't need a guide.

They received more than a few curious looks from the people they passed until something about Sevana would trigger their memories and they'd recall who she was. Then she received more than a few respectful bows, and once she spied a familiar face through a doorway, a child that she had brought in only four days ago. The boy waved with a grin, and she waved back, pleased that he was so openly delighted about his new home.

As they walked, she really explored with her senses her new surroundings. Synesthesia was a very unique experience and she looked around her eagerly, seeing what the world looked like through different senses. The world under the ocean waves was one of bold colors, beautifully arranged, like an undersea garden. Especially here, in the residential district of the city, people cultivated a wide variety of soft corals and feather duster worms, often lining their beds with sea urchins. It made for a beautiful palette of bold golds, deep reds, feathery lavenders, and stark whites, mixed in with the earthen tones of the sea urchins. To Sevana, whose sense of taste was quite strong at the moment, it was like taking her tongue on a stroll through a banquet. Sometimes she'd pause and stare at something a little longer, either to figure out why the taste was familiar—the thin, light green sea anemones that stood tall like grass tasted oddly like cucumber—but sometimes because it tasted so lovely that she wanted to give it a few more figurative licks. Tasting the colors, poking at the scents wafting around her, made her feel like she was in a different dimension altogether. For a moment, Sevana could ignore the uncertainties plaguing her and bask in the discovery of a world askew from the one she knew.

Aran paced alongside her, both amused and disturbed by what she reported, although eventually he saw the humor in it and smiled along with her. Sevana watched him out of the corner of her eye as they walked, her mind caught on a question. Really, it was a question that she should have asked long before this one: What had sparked this flawless devotion? No matter what happened, how irritable she became, how dangerous the situation turned, the one constant in her life since the Fae tracker had stepped into it was Aran. Sevana could not be more sure of her own shadow than she was of him.

The loyalty and affection were obvious enough, but the motivation escaped her utterly. What was it about her that had drawn Aran so strongly to her side? Why was he attracted when she repelled most others? It made no sense whatsoever.

It wasn't a complaint—far from it. Sevana might not understand him, but the thought of him leaving gave her chills. Her world had undergone a paradigm shift without her conscious decision to incorporate Aran into it. The idea of going forward without his companionship was unbearable. Last night, waking to find him still next to her, willing to give her any comfort to ease her through the nauseating pain, had made that very clear to her. But now that she had this knowledge, what was she supposed to do with it?

Emotions were so incredibly difficult. Sevana wished that she could outsource it, somehow scoop them all into a bowl and present them to Aran and demand: 'Just what is this because it's very strange and I think it's your fault?'

They rounded the bend before she could decide to ask or not and saw the main engine house for the transportation tubes. It was and wasn't as Sevana expected: a large sea cave that had been adapted over, the front part of it immersed in the air bubble, although clearly most of the area past wasn't. The three starfish stuck to the air barrier made that amply clear. Three tubes formed of smooth rock sat with the opening facing the street, a flat circular set of benches resting inert inside each tube, awaiting passengers. Sevana hazarded a guess that it would mean someone would have to apply a protective coating around the seats for their passengers to safely pass through the tubes until the light caught the angle just so and she realized that there was in fact a round shell sitting under the benches, and signs that a top part rested on the other side. So the tops were just off for now? That made more sense. A simple air bubble would not be protective enough for high speed travel down the tubes.

An Unda in human form wandered out, a book in his hands that he absently checked through, but on spying them he stopped dead. "Are you perhaps Artifactor Sevana Warren?"

"I am," she confirmed, stepping forward and giving him a respectful nod of the head. He looked mid-thirties, but the Unda did not age, much like the Fae. He could be hundreds of years old and this deceptive look of smooth skin and stout body not actually an indication of his age. "This is Arandur."

He ducked his head in a lower bow than she'd given him. "Pleasure. I'm Loman, head engineer. I've got one assistant engineer here with me today, Pol, but he's checking something in the back. I'll introduce you later."

"Just you two?"

"We sent our other two technicians out along the lines," Loman explained. "We ran a short test last night, and we're double-checking the results this morning."

That sounded promising. Sevana loved data. "Start with the problem itself. All Rane told me was that the tubes were having trouble, they only worked intermittently, and for the most part people had stopped using them."

Loman's expression went pinched and vexed. "You agreed to help with such little information? Bless you, then, as I've explained the problem more in-depth than that to our queen. The problem, Artifactor, is that we don't know what the problem is. Our transportation tubes are a complex highway that connects with five other clans. We go as far as the northern section of Belen, and we're the most southern clan that it sees. For many generations, the system has worked fine. A few hiccups here or there, but we always found the problem and resolved it. Then, strangely, about twenty years ago we started experiencing trouble. The clan past the Kesly Isles was the first to experience it. The tubes ran fine as far as we could tell, but the passengers would get stuck partway. They'd just stop dead; we mounted more than one rescue party before we were forced to shut them down."

Sevana's mind raced with possibilities. "And then?"

"And then the trouble started on our side as well," he continued, grimacing. "People were getting stuck partway. Then it took an unexpected turn, where sometimes they would shoot off into connecting tunnels, even though the system wasn't opened to that. They'd wind up deities-knows-where and it was quite the hassle getting them back again. I ran several tests myself, but aside from identifying two different tunnels that were proven to be problematic—although I don't know how—we couldn't determine the reason. I shut it down myself. Short distances seem to be fine, but if we go past the reef barrier—" he turned to gesture towards the distant horizon, an area just off the coast of Sa Kao "—then we have trouble more than half the time."

"Can I see your engine?"

"Of course." Loman promptly turned and led the way inside.

The engine inside didn't look like something that a human engineer would create. It didn't have gears, or large blocks of metal, or anything along those lines. Iron in water rusted quickly, and Sevana hadn't expected the Unda to use anything machine-related. What did meet her eyes was something altogether different. Ancient pressure valves lined the walls, each one directly connected with a hard-pressure lever and a screen of glass that showed a very complicated graph of intersecting lines in different colors. Sevana couldn't begin to read the writing on that glass, and not just because it was cramped and tiny, but in a language so old she couldn't even identify it.

But she didn't actually need to read it to be able to determine the basics. Each tube directly connected to a single destination, and the glass outlined the tubes it took to reach that particular place.

This system kept water entirely out, the tubes meant only to hold air. The lever activated seals on the tubes, building up the air pressure necessary in order to propel the pod inside forward. It was a simple, very workable concept.

"How many destinations from this point?" she inquired of Loman.

"Eighteen," he answered respectfully, mouth turning up slightly in a pleased expression. He apparently realized she didn't need a basic explanation.

"I realize that the two of you know what's going on, but someone explain it to me," Aran requested dryly. "I'm not trained in this."

"System's not that complex," Sevana assured him with an airy wave at the damp walls. "It goes like this: Each lever that you see connects to a different set of tubes, and a different destination. When the lever is engaged, all of the air inside the tube is suctioned out, creating a vacuum, which gives it enough pressure to propel the pod inside forward. That energy is maintained until the pod arrives, then someone on the other end releases the pressure to end the vacuum inside the tube and the passengers can exit. The problem is that something's gone wrong in the past few decades; there's no longer sustainable pressure, hence why some of the tubes that are connected are sucking in unwary passengers. Or they just get stuck midway."

"We've run every possible test on the system at the various stations, but none of the engines seem to have any issues," Loman added, frustration evident in his voice and the way he flung his hand up. "But it must be here somewhere, as the short tests that we run work just fine. It's only when we go past the reef, or any other real distance, that the pod stops dead. Or we end up in a side tube."

Sevana rocked back and forth on her heels, mind spinning madly as she looked the controls over carefully. "My Master is very fond of saying that complex systems fail in complex ways. Still, as integrated as all of this is, your engine itself isn't complex. You've been running regular diagnostics and tests on this since the beginning, haven't you? And the tubes are maintaining their air tight seals, you haven't found any signs of leakage?" She didn't need Loman's weary nod to answer the question, that much was obvious. "I think it's rather obvious, the problem isn't in here."

"But it must be," he protested heatedly, voice growing louder. "We're not sustaining pressure—"

She cut him off with a shake of the head. "You're wrong. If the problem was here, someone would have spotted it already. And it's very clear to me, it can't be here anyway. Yours wasn't the first station to fail, you just told me that. How can two stations, not directly connected to each other, fail at the same time?"

Loman closed his mouth with a snap and stared at her, almost belligerent. "You know what's happening?"

"Not yet," Sevana admitted cheerfully.

Aran snorted and explained to the bristling engineer, "Don't take her attitude to heart. She loves a good challenge. I think you just handed her one. Even though she says that, I know that expression. She's got at least one or two ideas of what's actually gone wrong."

Sevana grinned up at him. He did know her so well. "First step, let's go check out the really troublesome tube."

Giving her an unamused look, Aran half-growled, "You want to walk outside and inspect the tubes while your senses are playing tricks on you."

Put like that, it did sound like a bad idea, didn't it? "Who knows, maybe that will come in handy. If nothing else, I can use your eyes and ears. Come on, Aran, chop chop. There's a puzzle to unravel and no time to waste."

Aran muttered something under his breath that did not sound at all flattering.

Not waiting on him, Sevana tugged Loman into motion. "You'll need to create an air bubble for me, and we can't go far—I'm due back in this evening—but I'd like to at least start in on this. What's the best way to inspect the tube line?"

Loman, at least, seemed happy with her attitude to dive right in, and immediately drew her in the right direction. Aran followed, still grumbling, although he sounded more resigned now.

Really, what did he expect her to do when she had such a lovely problem to sink her teeth into?

Loman directed them to actually climb inside the tunnel and walk the interior first, which Sevana happily did. She inspected every ounce of the walls, taking her time with it, not interested in going at a quick pace. The walls were formed of hardened stone, utterly smooth to the touch, with practically mechanical precision. If ever Sevana needed proof that the Fae had infinitesimal control over the elements, this alone would do it. The walls were not coral, not as most of the buildings constructed in the city, but basalt. Theoretically, Sevana had known that most of the sea floor was made of basalt—the multitude of volcanoes made that inevitable—but seeing so much of the fine-grained volcanic rock in one place still bemused her. It was so incredibly, unapologetically black, as deep a color as sin itself. The only thing giving off any light were the florescent minerals someone had crushed and painted along the insides.

She touched the walls several times with her bare hands, which felt strange in her state, as the walls tasted cool, damp and earthy, but touching them mixed sensation in with it. It wasn't unlike biting into a dark pumpernickel bread and finding gravel inside. "I assume that the round shape of the tunnel is designed to give the bubble pods perfect pressure?"

"Yes, Artifactor," Loman confirmed easily over his shoulder. He paused to watch her, his eyes calculating and wondering. Whatever he thought of her, he chose to keep it to himself. "We crafted them specifically so that the tunnel dimensions would measure just an inch on all sides to give the pod clearance."

Aran let out a low whistle. "That's not much at all. Why that close?"

"The pressure," Sevana explained absently over her shoulder. "In order to propel the pod forward, it requires a certain amount of pressure around the pod, and that's best achieved by giving it a very slim margin of space on all sides. It's really quite ingenious. It takes almost no magic to run this, and yet it's swift, efficient, and perfectly safe to use. If I could somehow adapt this for human magicians to use, I'd make a bloody fortune."

"Focus, Sev," Aran drawled. He put his hand next to hers on the wall, frowning at it. "I really don't sense any seepage of water through the walls. What are you looking for?"

"Something wrong." When that got her a flat look from both men, Sevana shrugged. "What do you want me to say? The pressure gauges at the engine room report that the pressure inside the tubes is stable, as always. There's no change there. If it's not a problem of maintaining pressure, it had to be a problem here. There *has* to be something here that has been overlooked. I won't know what it is until I see it."

Making a 'let's keep walking' gesture with his hand, Aran walked on.

They walked and walked, mostly in silence. Sevana had every sense, magical and otherwise, trained on the walls around her. She didn't expect to see something that the men would miss, but at the same time, she couldn't help but focus. The puzzle of this problem had drawn her attention very strongly. Sevana never could resist a good challenge; she loved to sharpen her mind against such problems, but even she could admit that part of this was ego. Unda engineers had been struggling with this issue for the past twenty years. It would be quite the feat if she could succeed where they had failed.

As much as she focused on the tunnel, however, it did not escape her notice that Aran paid strict attention to her. At the first sign of fatigue or distress, she had no doubt that he'd scoop her up and cart her back to Ursilla. Part of her bristled at being treated like some delicate piece of fluff, but the practical part of her pointed out that he had every right to be concerned. Cramming a transformation that should take at least ten years into a six-week period was bad enough, but her body had already proven resistant. He had cause to be concerned.

Despite her senses playing havoc with her, Sevana didn't feel under the weather. Not like yesterday, when her body shuddered so badly it felt like it was breaking apart. Anything was better than that. It felt good, actually, to be able to walk out and stretch her legs a little, to have her mind sharply in focus instead of curled up in animalistic pain like the day before. Hopefully she wouldn't be reduced to that again. Her only problem at the moment was something else entirely. Because every color smelled like food to her, she felt strangely full, as if she'd been indulging herself by snacking all day. Her stomach, however, complained, as it knew very well that she hadn't been eating, only smelling and tasting. It was an odd dichotomy of sensations.

They walked all the way to the reefs—or so Loman claimed, Sevana couldn't begin to tell through the thick stone walls—and then a little further. Sevana stared at the spot where their pods always got stuck and couldn't discern a bit of difference between one patch of wall and the next. Nor did she really expect to with her bare eyes. If it was obvious, someone would have spotted it before her.

"She'll want to come back tomorrow with proper measuring tools, with any blueprints you have of the tunnels, and then run some short tests," Aran informed Loman factually.

With those very words on the tip of her tongue, Sevana paused, blinking up at him. Did he really know her that well? Apparently so. "Yes, what he said. Also, Loman, when we get back I want to examine the pod from this tunnel. It's normally the same pod that runs back and forth, correct?"

"Yes, that's correct." Loman's dark eyes narrowed suspiciously. "You think you know what's happening."

"Hmm, I have a hunch, I will say that. Recent events on my last case have cast a suspicion at me, shall we say." Turning on her heels, she gestured for them to go back. "Nothing I can say without proper measurements and some diagnostics, though. I don't suppose you have wands down here? Measuring tapes? Anything along those lines?"

They talked tools—which was educational in its own right—on the way back, Loman becoming more agreeable with every step as she outlined her plan of what she wanted to test next. At this point, the man's pride didn't care if it got battered about, as long as they finally solved the problem. Sevana knew that feeling well.

6

Sevana, Loman, and Aran made it back to the tube's entrance, only to be curtailed in their examination of the pod by Ursilla. The elderly Unda stood just outside the tube with her arms crossed over her chest, one finger tapping out an impatient staccato on her arm. Her expression looked exactly like a mother who'd told the children not to go out and play, only to find that they'd done so anyway—and were covered in mud, to boot.

Sevana, not at all deterred by that expression, gave her an airy wave. "Hello. Waiting on me, I take it."

"Yes." Ursilla gave her an elaborate once over. "Not that you're late, but I dropped by to examine you and see how you fared, only to find that you'd gone out. To work, no less. Because, of course, it makes sense to work when one was doubled over in pain and experiencing high fevers the day before."

The woman's tone was so incredibly peeved that Sevana couldn't contain her snicker. "I feel much better today. Although my senses are a little screwy and muscles are still aching a mite."

"By that she means that everything is either switched around or connected to each other," Aran translated. He, too, seemed a little exasperated with Sevana and in perfect sympathy with Ursilla in that moment. "She's tasting colors, touching scents, and probably something else that she hasn't bothered to mention."

With a casual shrug, Sevana decided to tweak their noses even further and denied brightly, "It really is only those two. Although

I think it would be amazing if my sight and hearing somehow got mixed up together. Wouldn't that be amazing? I'm not sure how it would work, though."

Ursilla noted to Aran, "She's baiting us."

"She does that. She has a very terrible sense of humor sometimes. Ursilla, this synesthesia, you mentioned it only as a possibility. How long did it last, the previous times you changed someone?"

"A few days." Ursilla shifted her stance to something more relaxed. She likely felt calmer after finally finding her quarry safe and, for the most part, alright. "I can't be specific, as each person is different, and Sellion's magic is directly tied into her senses. It will probably take longer to adjust them because of that."

Sevana didn't mind the changed-up senses. In fact, it was rather unique and educational—as long as she didn't lose them entirely. That would put her in a bind, make her even more dependent on another's help, and she loathed that idea with every fiber of her being.

Loman had been hovering nearby during this exchange, and he asked uncertainly, "Are you unable to work any further today, Artifactor?"

"It appears so." Sevana turned to speak with him directly. "Loman, you've got those blueprints of the tunnels and the engine on hand, don't you?"

"They're actually held in Archives over in the library," he corrected.

"Get those out and send them to my guest house," she requested/ordered. "I'll want to study those, assuming that I can think after my treatment today. I feel like there's something very obvious that we're all missing, although I can't quite put my finger on what."

"I'll do so," he promised faithfully. "Good luck?"

Growling, she headed for Ursilla. "I'll need it. See you when I can think again."

"We'll be waiting."

Ursilla led the way back down the street, informing Sevana and Aran as they walked, "I'm glad to see that you've adjusted as well as you have. We'll do another treatment but this time lower, on the back of the neck. It's vital that we start to alter the nervous system."

The walk to the guest house was less pleasant than before, as uneasy anticipation stewed in her gut at the idea of another treatment. She grimly set her jaw, already marshalling her determination to get her through the rest of the day.

They almost bumped into Khan as they entered the guest house. Her young host was coming out with a stack of laundry in his hands, mostly the bedsheets from her bed, by the look of it. He paused and gave her a nod of the head, the best he could do with his hands full. "Artifactor. I changed the sheets. You have a cold lunch of shrimp salad waiting for you on the table, and crab stuffed baguettes for snacks. Is there anything else that I can bring you?"

"More ice," she requested instantly. With the treatment coming up, she just knew she'd be experiencing hot flashes and probably fevers as well.

"Understood. I'll be back shortly." Khan gave her another duck of the head before hurrying off in a ground-eating stride.

They went in, and this time Sevana didn't need to do as much to give Aran the room to work with. She gathered up her hair and tied it in a loose knot at the top of her head, exposing her neck to him, then lowered the collar enough that he could reach the skin without putting blood on the cloth. His finger was once again gentle and precise as he drew the emblem on her bare skin. Sevana knew that to be the general area where a great many nerve endings gathered, so expected the application of blood there to be less than pleasant.

Great dark magic, did she ever underestimate that.

Her entire back felt on fire, muscles knotting and contracting at the conflicting signals it received, and for some reason she underwent a severe attack of vertigo. So severe that it almost emptied her stomach more than once. Sevana was glad that she hadn't actually eaten lunch before this treatment, as it certainly would have come up by now. Arandur moved her to the bed to help with the vertigo, and Ursilla lingered for a time to keep an eye on her, but there wasn't much to be done until her body absorbed it. Eventually the elderly Unda left with promises to check in again later.

It was just as well that she'd requested more ice from Khan, as she ended up curled on the bed, ice packs pressed against her back to keep her body from becoming one huge blister. Aran, thankfully, knew better than to hover and found ways to be nearby without being intrusive about it. Just as well, as Sevana's crankiness rose every minute and if he tried smothering her, she'd have ripped his head off. Being helpless and in pain was not her forte.

With her body spasming, she didn't have the brainpower to work on the transportation problem. Pity, that. Sevana could have used the distraction; it truly was an interesting problem. Why would something hundreds of years old, and well-maintained, suddenly fail? Fail in multiple areas, no less.

Unfortunately, that was as far as she could think. Anything more complex than that went spiraling out into the void.

"Sevana?" Aran sank next to her on the mattress, where she lay curled up on her bed. "Tashjian sent a response back. Want me to read it to you?"

She did not have the power of concentration available to make words out on paper right now. "Please."

"Alright." The crinkle of paper, of a wax seal being snapped open, then Aran cleared his throat before starting, "Sweetling, I just got your note. I have to say, while I did see this coming, I'm not truly happy to hear it. Are you sure this is the right course? We've not exhausted the human experts, there might be a way yet to remove the Fae blood in you and leave you fully human."

Aran tried to read this neutrally but she could hear the strain, the hint of upset in his voice as he conveyed her master's words to her. Aran did not at all agree with that.

"I want you to stop and really think about it before you go any further," Master's letter continued. "Sarsen's been dispatched to Big to help shut your business down, as you asked. He's agreed to help Morgan fulfill any outstanding contracts, and I don't have to tell you that you owe him quite the favor for that, do I? Take your time, think about matters. Don't worry about things here, we have it handled."

Sevana let out a gusty sigh, her eyes slipping closed for a moment.

She'd more or less predicted half of that letter.

The paper rustled again as Aran set it aside. He adjusted the cold packs along her back, fingers gentle as he worked. "Should we stop?"

"No point," Sevana responded wearily. "He doesn't know it, but I contacted every person that I thought would know something while I was still lying in bed recovering. No one knew anything helpful. A few people requested that I keep them updated, as they wanted to know how I turned out. There's no human experts that can help." Heaving a gusty sigh, she stared blindly at the multi-colored wall in front of her. "He's just worried, always has been."

"He's not the only one."

Sevana was tempted to turn her head so she could see Aran's expression. The next twinge of pain shooting along her spine discouraged the idea of moving. "Can't blame me for that, Aran. This situation is too strange and I was thrown into it without any chance to prepare."

A ruminative silence followed for a few seconds. "You…Did you make this decision because you didn't feel like there was another option?"

"There isn't another option. Not a good option, at least."

"Sevana, I hate for you to think that this is simply the lesser evil."

He sounded truly perturbed by that. And Sevana hadn't really meant her decision was the lesser of two evils, although in a sense that was the case. She dared to turn her head just enough to catch his eye. Aran leaned over her back, green eyes clouded with concern, an unhappy downwards turn of his mouth as he watched her. Sevana didn't want to leave him with that impression. "It's not…well, it is. But it isn't."

"Yes, that clarified things nicely," he responded dryly.

A tired smile flicked over her face. "I mean, I can't stay as I am. I can't try removing your blood, it will only half-work. Living like this the rest of my life, where I can't work, where I can't even function day-to-day without something melting or exploding on me, would drive me mad. The only sensible option was to go forward."

Aran stroked her arm gently, slumping in on himself. "I had a feeling that was your logic. But Sellion, the world that awaits you isn't to be feared. You don't need to be…I'm not sure what you are. Are you nervous? You don't seem to look forward to it."

"I don't think being Fae will be terrible," she assured him huskily. Thirst scratched at her throat. She'd have to move in a few minutes and get some water. Just lying here the rest of the night wouldn't help her recover. "I never thought that."

"But you don't look forward to it, either. You hold firmly onto your human connections."

"Of course I do. I'm not done with the human world yet. I don't think I ever will be completely." She nearly left it at that but Aran… of all people, he could likely understand her, assuming she could find the right words to express herself. "The one thing that I fear is that Aranhil will want to keep me tightly inside of South Woods. He's already making noises about that."

"You don't want to live with us?"

"No…yes?" Sevana growled to herself. She truly was terrible at expressing sentiment. "I don't want to leave Big."

Aran paused, his hand falling motionless on her arm. "Is that what it is? You don't want to leave your friend?"

"Of course. Isn't that obvious?"

Something that might have been a snort of amusement left him. "We don't read minds, Sellion. Is it just Big that you don't want to separate from?"

"Well, I want to stay with my human friends for as long as I have them." Sevana thought that obvious, too, but apparently not. "And I'm not good at staying holed up in one place, you know that. I need puzzles, challenges, work that demands my talents. I can't just stay in South Woods day in and day out, I'll eventually go mad with boredom."

"Heavens forbid," Aran responded jokingly. "Alright, I understand your hesitation now. But Sevana, I think you've jumped to conclusions you should not have. We spend a decade, sometimes more, preparing our children to step into the Fae world. We are rushing your transformation now because we fear for your health and safety. But none of us wish to rush your entrance into South Woods. Of course you will need time to adjust."

That all sounded fine and dandy but it didn't match what Aranhil had said to her before. "Aranhil wants me in South Woods, though."

"He fears for your safety and would rather have you close," Aran admitted calmly. "But if you explain to him that you do not wish to lose contact with your friends yet, he will be patient. When you live as long as we do, you do not consider time in any increment shorter than decades. The time you need is not significant to us."

Well. Put like that. Sevana felt the weight of worry slip off her shoulders, just a mite. "You really think Aranhil won't throw a fit about me living in Big?"

"It might take some compromise," Aran admitted ruefully. "He *is* very excited about having you properly one of us. Just be firm about your needs, Sellion. He will acknowledge them."

Funny, how he only used her Fae name in moments like these. His advice was good, though. Sevana had only put her foot down, she hadn't explained what she wanted or why, and it was hard to compromise with a person that didn't try to explain anything. She needed to rectify that. "When I can sit up without my eyes spinning, I'll write him a proper letter outlining what I need. Maybe a timeline, too."

"That is an excellent plan. Do that." His weight shifted but did not lift off the bed. "You sound thirsty. Can you sit up and drink something?"

"Hopefully."

"I might be able to locate a straw. Let's try turning you instead, let you recline as much as possible."

She nodded in relief, as that sounded much more workable. As he drew away from the bed, a thought occurred. "You realize that when I tell Aranhil that I want to stay in Big for a while, he's likely going to make you live with me."

Aran's expression was a soft mix of amusement and affection. "Tell me something I don't know."

Alright, that might have been an obvious statement. She watched him leave, considering what that really meant. No one had ever wanted to live with her. Not for long stretches of time. The only two who had managed it were Master and Sarsen, and they had many a tale to share with the unwary about how challenging it had been to share the same roof with her. But Aran, having seen her at her absolute worst, didn't think anything of living with her for potentially decades?

A strange thrill went through her, an emotion she normally didn't feel tugging at her heart strings. It wasn't pleasure, or contentment, or happiness, or anticipation—it seemed to be a mix of all of those things, an emotional gestalt that she couldn't clearly define. Normally the idea of having someone else constantly underfoot in her space irritated her, but somehow Aran was the exception.

Decades with him. She looked forward to it.

7

The next day Sevana felt better. Ineligible for burial within the next twenty-four hours type of better, not springing out of bed better. She managed to get out of bed and, finally, eat something without instantly spewing it back up, which were all pluses. She'd take 'em.

Sevana, with some help, moved from bed to couch, although the cold packs stayed on her back. The twinges of pain might keep her from wandering around outside, but it did not prohibit her from working. But first thing first: make sure a war hadn't broken out.

Tapping the finger on her mirror's surface, she called, "Milly."

Aran came to kneel next to the chair, touching her arm lightly. "Will you be alright for a while? I want to go get more ice."

The last of it being currently pressed up against her spine and neck, she knew why. "Sure. Go, get some fresh air. I'll likely be stuck in diplomatic talks, assuming I can reach Master and Aranhil."

Relieved, he gave a nod, hand squeezing her fingers briefly before pulling on his boots and walking through the door. Knowing that Milly was likely somewhere else entirely, Sevana patiently tapped the mirror again. "Milly."

Someone with a light, female voice stopped Aran and spoke with him outside. Sevana's ears perked, but she didn't dare turn her head. Moving that appendage currently brought about pain. But the voice was a familiar one. Sevana couldn't quite place it, but she knew it.

"Hello, Artifactor? It's Kira."

Kira. Oh, right, Rane's right hand. She hadn't seen Kira recently, not since her first approach into Living Waters territory—actually, when she'd been chasing two goddesses. "Come in, Kira. All the way, I can't turn my head just now."

"Yes, so your companion explained." Kira skipped around into view, looking unfairly freshly put together. Her dark hair hung in silky waves around her shoulders, the white dress flowing about her in an elegant style that matched the pearls threaded through her hair. She gave Sevana a sympathetic smile. "I'm actually your next-door neighbor, of sorts. I live across the street."

In the five days that Sevana had been here, she hadn't seen her, but that didn't mean much. Likely their schedules were entirely different. "Are you checking in on me, then?"

"I am. Rane asked me to keep an eye on you. Khan is a dear child, but he's not very experienced with Landers, and there might be things he can't anticipate you'll need." Head canting to the side, she eyed Sevana thoughtfully. "It looks as if the treatments are working, at least."

"Yes, they are. Fortunately." Sevana was of the opinion that the treatments had better work, as she wasn't going through all of this without something to show for it. "And Khan's doing fine. He's quick to fetch things as we need them."

The way that Kira smiled, mostly in relief, suggested to Sevana that Khan was either a friend or a relative of some sort. "Good. I'm glad to hear it. I'm to report to Rane and Curano in a moment; is there anything I should pass along to them?"

Sevana almost said no, then thought better of it. "Tell them that I have gone and looked at the transportation system. I at least have a better grasp on the problem now. I'll work the problem as I can."

Nodding understanding, Kira gestured at the door. "I'll do that. Let me know if you need anything."

"I will." Sevana almost watched her go out of habit, then thought better of it when her abused neck muscles twinged. She tracked Kira by ear as she left. So Rane's trusted assistant lived across the street from her, eh? Sevana didn't for one moment think that coincidental. Perhaps Rane wanted to just keep an eye on her, but Sevana suspected other reasons were at play as well.

"Sevana?"

She blinked and focused on the mirror propped up against the wall. Milly's round face stared back at her. "Milly. There you are."

"My dear, you do not look well," Milly informed her frankly, expression growing pinched with worry.

"This is one of the reasons why I like you," Sevana responded dryly. "You lay everything on the table. The treatments are a little harsh, to put it mildly. But I'm coping well enough. I got a letter from Master, but I'd hoped to speak to him directly. Has he managed to figure out a way to connect the mirrors?"

"Oh, yes, we ran a trial version last night. I have to help him, but it's possible to connect four at once. No more than that, though. It's too taxing on me to do more than four."

Tapping a thoughtful finger to her lips, Sevana opined, "I believe four's all we need. Tell him that I want to connect the Sa Kaoan king, Aranhil, and myself today to speak. His last letter to me didn't mention anything about reparations between Aranhil and Sa Kao, and I don't want the loss of the Institute to lead to bad blood."

Milly nodded fervently. "We all wish to avoid that. I'll tell him. Today?"

"If we can. I'm clear-headed enough to speak today, but these treatments either lay me flat out or barely make me twinge. It's hard to predict."

With a determined nod, Milly assured her, "I'll contact everyone and set it up. You stay right there."

Heaven forbid that anyone cross her determined friend. The thought amused her and she picked up the blueprints lying nearby, studying them thoughtfully. On paper, at least, nothing jarred. The tunnels followed the plans to a T and didn't deviate from her own examination yesterday. Still, something niggled at the back of her mind. Something was off there….

"Sweetling."

Blinking, she looked up and this time she saw Master's reflection. Not like she saw Milly, with her disembodied form, but a true reflection of the man relaxing in his favorite armchair near a flickering fireplace. He did not look entirely at his ease, elbows propped up on his knees, the wrinkles in his face more pronounced than normal.

Glad to see him, she offered a smile. "Hi, Master. I got your letter."

"I'm glad, but sweetling, you look like something Baby dragged in."

"Feel like it too," she admitted ruefully. "But still, we're making progress. It turns out that the woman who's changing me has done it twice before."

Master let out a pent-up breath. "So she has successful experience. I'm relieved to hear that, sweetling. And after you've changed?"

"Aran assures me that while Aranhil will want to drag me straight into South Woods, they'll respect my wishes. Likely someone from my new family will need to live with me for a while in Big, but I won't disappear altogether." She paused, waiting to see if that was the reassurance he needed.

Master's frown did not fade, as she'd hoped, but rather deepened. "You're set on this course, then?"

"Ursilla informs me that she can strip the Fae blood out of me. But it won't fix my unbalanced magical core and will shorten my life considerably. Which would you prefer, Master?"

Tashjian sighed gustily, like a blacksmith's bellows. "Put like that, it is the only sensible option. Alright, if you're sure? Of course you are."

"I wouldn't be going through this much pain and nausea and general unpleasantness if I was anything shy of absolute certainty," she assured him drolly. "I assume that while we're chatting, Milly's helping you set up the other two?"

"Yes, she managed to find both other men and they agreed to speak now."

Sevana had worried that, as short notice as it was, they wouldn't be able to choreograph four people speaking at the same time. But then again, surely the other two had their own agendas to push regarding the incident and dropped everything to accommodate her.

That was far more likely. "While we wait, I have another question for you. Since I'll be stuck down here for another five weeks or so, do you want me to grab anything for you and Sarsen?"

"Merciful heavens, child, but if you're offering me souvenirs, I'll take them. You sure that you're up to gathering them for me?"

"Even if I'm not, I can use it as an excuse to get Aran out of the house. He'll likely need breaks from me sooner or later."

In complete understanding, Master nodded in support of this. "Good plan. Have something to write down on?"

Sevana dutifully took notes on the very, very long shopping list. At least part of this must be for Sarsen. Or it better be for Sarsen. She wasn't hauling more than this home again. Master barely had it all out before Milly connected another mirror with hers, the image splitting so that it was exactly in half, Master on the right, Aranhil on the left. Her new king/father figure lit up in a smile as he saw her.

"Daughter, I can see the changes even from here. But you look very tired," he noted, smile faltering.

"It's not pleasant, doing this so quickly, but we're making progress," she answered forthrightly. "And Aran's barely left my side during all of this. I'm managing."

As if her words had summoned him, Aran returned, a bucket making heavy sloshing noises as he moved through the room. "Ah, I see your plan worked. Aranhil, Tashjian, how are you?"

"Well," Aranhil assured him.

"Thank you for taking care of her, Arandur." Tashjian's voice and expression was transparent with sincerity.

"It is my pleasure," Aran assured him. "Sev, do you need more ice?"

Grimacing, she admitted, "I think I just have water against my back right now."

"Let me have the packs, then." Putting the bucket down, he gently levered out the oiled skin packs and carted them all into the kitchen.

Firuz Adnan, King of Sa Kao, appeared and split the image of the mirror again. Now it was in three quadrants, with him on the bottom third, sharing space with the others. It looked a little odd, and she could barely see more than his head and shoulders, but it would suffice for their purposes. He looked impeccable, white turban and feather stiffly correct on his head, black beard combed, the purple sash around his shoulders silently indicating his royalty. "Artifactor. I am relieved to see you are unharmed."

"No thanks to your subjects," Aranhil grumbled with a dark look.

A tic jumped at the corner of Firuz's mouth. "I believe you more than claimed your revenge for that incident, King of South Woods."

"Boys, don't fight," Sevana grumbled. "For one, I'm not in the mood to mediate, and for another, I don't see why the victim should be the voice of reason in the room. If anyone deserves the right to bash heads together, it's me."

"She has a point there," Master observed to the other two, more than a little smug about it. "King Adnan, I assume that you knew nothing about the kidnapping?"

Firuz unbent enough to admit, "No. They did not inform anyone of their intentions. Of course, if I had known, I would have prevented it—or at least taken steps to inform her properly first. The way this matter was handled…does not reflect well."

Triumphant, Aranhil observed, "Then you have no objections to our actions."

"But," Firuz added pointedly, "I do not agree with the way you handled the matter. You destroyed the Institute to the point that not even the foundation remains. Several people died as the building collapsed."

Aranhil gave a casual shrug. "You kidnapped our daughter. Any fool who does such will be met with blood and violence. It is our way."

Sevana closed her eyes, a sinking feeling reminding her of the lives that had been lost that day. Still, that was about the reaction she expected from a Fae. They were scarily ruthless when wronged. Before she could open her mouth, Firuz jumped right back in.

"But she isn't harmed," Firuz argued heatedly. "Make no mistake, I owe this woman a great deal. She restored my daughter to me, she helped several of my citizens regain themselves, and I wish no harm upon her. But still, she wasn't harmed when she was taken. You destroyed a magical research facility that does—did—much for my country. For the world."

"She wasn't harmed because my cousins, the Unda, rescued her before your magicians had a chance to do anything to her," Aranhil riposted, voice rising with each word. "You cannot claim with certainty what would have happened to her if she'd stayed there any longer!"

Sevana grew impatient with this argument, as they could go in circles for hours, and clapped her hands sharply. "Again, the victim should not be the voice of reason in the room. Firuz, I well understand your agitation, as I share it. The Institute was a place well known for learning. But it's water under the bridge now—the building can't be revived, nor can the dead walk out of their graves. They made a very stupid mistake and, unfortunately, paid for it. Even you agreed it was a stupid thing to do. Will you defend their stupidity?"

Part of Firuz really wanted to argue yes, but he visibly bit it back. "No. No, I cannot do that. For your sake, I truly cannot. But I cannot just dismiss this matter either, Sevana."

"Nor should you. Your country was invaded without a by-your-leave; at the very least, an apology is owed for that." Turning her eyes up to the left section of the mirror, she grimaced a smile, the best she could do with this level of heat and pain searing at the back of her neck. "Aranhil. Do I need to tell you to play nice?"

The king of the Fae stared back at her, entirely unamused. "You are cheeky, daughter. Are you truly not upset with all of this?"

"The Institute was destroyed right down to the ground. What more revenge can I ask for?" she retorted calmly. "And really, you've almost gone to war with Sa Kao once before because of a misunderstanding. Do you want to repeat that mistake yet a second time?"

A little growl of frustration rumbled from the back of his throat. "Oh, very well. We will let bygones be bygones. Will a dozen Alder trees be sufficient as an apology?"

Master's eyebrows shot into his hairline, a mannerism that Sevana duplicated as she stared at Aranhil in surprise. The Alder tree was considered sacred among the Fae, as it was a symbol of resurrection and had the power of divination, especially in the diagnosing of diseases. It was sacrosanct; only a fool dared to cut it down.

"Firuz," Master directed urgently, "if you're not familiar with this tree, I will answer for you: take the deal. It's a very powerful tree and not one that the Fae choose to share with the outside world very often. It's by far a very excellent token for an apology."

Thankfully, Firuz was a king who could take counsel. He studied Master's expression for a moment, then Sevana's, before nodding slowly. "Very well. I will accept this."

"I will send someone to plant them in your palace grounds within the next fortnight," Aranhil promised reluctantly. "But be aware, we will not respond well to another breach of etiquette. My daughter wishes to remain in the human world even after she's fully adopted into the Fae. If she's visited with harm again, I will not take it well."

"If she's taken again, then I will help you punish the idiots," Firuz promised tartly. "Just alert me that you're doing so first. I don't want to be caught off-guard again."

That soothed Aranhil as nothing else had. He settled into a more non-antagonistic stance. "That I can safely promise."

Aran came back with the cold packs but stayed put, just out of range of the mirror. Sevana appreciated that he didn't advertise how bad off she was, waiting until the conversation was over. "Then, gentlemen, I'll go. I've other things that demand my attention here."

Firuz inclined his head to her. "Thank you for reaching out, Artifactor. We appreciate your assistance and formally apologize for what happened."

Wanting to cut this short, Sevana went with the succinct response: "Thank you."

Firuz disappeared, leaving only the other two. To Aranhil, Sevana directed, "I'll give you a more detailed report of how I'm doing, but not today. I need to lie down."

"Of course," Aranhil urged her with a worried expression. "You've done more than you should today. Go and rest. I can sort out the rest of it."

He'd better. Sevana only had so much diplomacy in her system and she'd used up the vast majority of it today. With a salute, she waved the men off and grabbed Aran's arm, using him to pull herself out of the chair. "Bed. Ice."

Carefully supporting her weight, Aran gently helped her to the bedroom, then lay the ice packs along her back, wrapped in towels to take the bitter cold edge off. She lay there, shivering from the dichotomy of hot and cold, mentally counting down the days.

At least she wouldn't return to the surface with a war brewing.

8

Sevana flailed awake in sheer, unadulterated panic.

The dream had been strange, fear-inducing, a nonsensical scenario where she was desperately trying to free herself of something, something dark and cloying, only to fail with every attempt and get stuck further. Her heart beat a drum in her ears, sweat clinging to her skin as her fight and flight instincts kicked in until she jerked upright, panting for breath.

Why was the room so dark?

It shouldn't be dark, even in the dead of night; the florescent minerals embedded into the walls gave off a faint glow. Why didn't she see that? Nothing seemed out of place, although her senses were still screwy—could she even trust them?

Her panic doubled again as her hand flew to her face, fingers checking that her eyes were open. But she couldn't feel her skin, just the pressure of something poking near her eye. She couldn't see—smell—feel—anything. Total sensory deprivation except, strangely, her ears. She could hear the deep breathing of her friend in the next room, the dull roar of the ocean all around them, and the delicate trickle of voices from outside. It was beyond unnerving, it was borderline terrifying. Why was she having this severe trouble with her senses *now*?!

It took two breaths before she could make her throat loosen enough from its constricted clench that she could get any air out. Another three before she could get an actual word. Sevana clawed for sanity, for control, because being like this, being this helpless, filled her with dread. Finally, she managed in a husky, strained voice: "Aran."

In an instant, she heard bedsheets flip over, the soft thud as his feet hit the cold tile floor. A dip on the bed—his weight—and then pressure on her arms, although her skin didn't register any sense of heat or tactile sensation. "Sevana? You called for me?"

"I…" Breathe. Don't just sit there, breathe. She had to communicate with him, she had to tell him the problem, otherwise he couldn't help her. Forcing herself to grasp the patience that she'd been forced to cultivate during a long convalescence, Sevana stamped down on her bewilderment and fright enough that she could talk. "I can't see."

The bed moved in a sharp jerk. Aran had startled? "Nothing at all?"

"It's just darkness. I can't feel anything, either. Hearing seems to be fine, and I'm not sure about taste." It cost her dearly to say those words evenly and her own ears still heard the barely restrained panic in her report.

In a rapid tone, he ordered firmly, "Do not move, I'll get Ursilla."

The bedsprings sprang back up as he leapt off and darted away.

With nothing to do, Sevana sat tautly in the silence. It felt heavy to her—claustrophobically so—and she felt panic eating away at her sanity. Never before in her life had she been this helpless and Sevana didn't care for the experience one whit. She forced herself to draw in a breath, hold it, release. Breathe in, hold it, release. She did that over and over, forcing herself to not panic, to not have an attack of some sort, as that wouldn't do anyone any good, least of all her.

It felt like an eternity. More likely it was minutes later when two different people entered, their feet slapping against the tile as they scurried inside, and someone else sat on the edge of the bed. Sevana only knew it wasn't Aran because the weight was different, lighter.

"Sevana, you can still hear me?" Ursilla inquired in a low, rough voice, probably from being awoken so abruptly.

She nodded, then felt foolish for the motion. "Yes."

"I see a great swirl of energies within you. I believe that the Fae blood is battling it out with your senses. Allow me to examine you for a moment."

Not expecting answers to just spew out of the woman's mouth, Sevana gave another nod, more curt this time. She felt someone else—Aran—sit behind her, hands bracing her shoulders. She leaned into the contact slightly, because despite not being able to feel it properly, it still comforted her. Marginally, at least.

It took a moment, long and tense, silent as a graveyard at midnight.

"I'm correct," Ursilla finally pronounced. She had a very smug note to her voice, a tone that Sevana recognized full well, as it was something that she employed often. Sevana found it completely irritating and now had an appreciation for the people who wanted to smack her. "The Fae blood is battling it out for the control of your senses. Especially your sight, as it is directly connected to your magical core, so of course it would be resistant to change. Your sense of touch too, I believe, is very integrated with your magic. I had not quite anticipated such events, but they are not a surprise, either. Another application of Arandur's blood, and I think we'll be able to overpower matters. Enough, at least, that your senses are once again restored. Whether they'll be elevated to a Fae's level we'll have to wait and see."

"At the moment I'm less concerned about Fae senses and more concerned with having mine back," Sevana gritted out between clenched teeth. Don't hit the woman, don't hit the woman, don't hit the woman.

"Arandur, if you will?" Ursilla directed him casually. "In the center of her forehead."

The two on the bed switched places and Aran had to step into the other room to fetch his dagger before he could prick his finger. Sevana had the dullest impression of a finger against her skin, although no other sense of heat, wetness, or anything else as he traced the symbol onto her. Whatever Ursilla said about touch being connected to her magical core, it related to her skin in general, not just what her hands touched.

As he finished, everyone sat still and waited for several taut moments. Sevana found herself holding her breath, but when minutes ticked by, she was forced to release it and draw another. "I don't think this is going to be a quick change."

"Apparently not," Ursilla agreed calmly. "I suggest sleeping. It will speed the process along."

More likely, it would keep Sevana from going insane while waiting for things to revert. Sevana did not think she'd be able to sleep in this state—in fact she was very sure of it—but it didn't hurt to try.

Aran's thoughts ran along the same line, and he inquired, "Perhaps a sleeping draught of some sort?"

"Yes, that's probably wise. It will ease her transition if she's able to sleep solidly for a few hours. I'll fetch one." Ursilla rose and was gone with a gentle swish of skirts.

"How are you doing?" Aran asked gently against her ear, his weight pressed lightly along her back.

"I really don't like this," she gritted back between clenched teeth. Forcing out an explosive breath, she admitted, "But we didn't expect this to be easy. I shouldn't be surprised."

"I think when you wake up in the dead of night with only half your senses working, you're at the very least allowed to be surprised." He slid both arms around her waist and drew her into a comforting hug. "I'm very glad I stayed here with you."

Sevana relaxed back into his arms, just for a moment. What would it have been like? To have been here, alone, with only relative strangers about her? Sevana wasn't much for company, she could frankly admit that she preferred her alone time, but even hypothetically going through this without a friendly face nearby unnerved her. It felt strange, a little uncomfortable to admit, but perhaps she should. Aran had turned his world upside down to accommodate her. And she owed him at least a word of thanks. "I'm glad you came with me too."

She could hear the smile in his voice when he responded. "Really? Despite my hovering?"

"At least you're not annoying about it. I would have killed either

Kip or Master by this point."

Aran snorted in amusement. "Seeing how they reacted last time, I wouldn't have blamed you."

With a swish of skirts, Ursilla entered once more. "Here. Take this, all in one go if you can manage it."

"Let me guess," Sevana held out her hand blindly, fingers closing around the cool, cylindrical shape pressed into it. "It tastes vile."

"All good medicine does. The body recovers faster to avoid drinking it further."

Sevana felt like she'd heard those words before. Actually, she was fairly certain she'd said them at some point in time. With a grimace, she braced herself and upended the vial all in one go. Even trying to not taste, just swallow, it was impossible to avoid the mix on her tongue. It tasted very strongly of squid ink, stewed kelp left to steep too long, and the overpowering brine of the sea. (And why her sense of taste now worked correctly was another mystery.) Grimacing, she forced herself to finish it before handing it back. "And how long will that keep me asleep?"

"A full eight hours, at least," Ursilla answered calmly.

That sounded blissful right now. In fact, she felt the medicine start its effects already; she grew slightly light-headed, even as her body relaxed into that pre-slumber mode. "Good."

"I'll be right here just in case," Aran promised her, gently sliding out so that she could lay back down.

The blankets and pillow welcomed her like a returned friend and she sighed as she relaxed into them. Still, anxiety had a grip on her mind, and she felt reassured that Aran would stay nearby. Absolutely nothing could get by that man, Sevana would bet her soul on that. "Aran."

"Hmm?"

"Don't just sit there watching me," she ordered fuzzily. Sevana had seen him do this before, where he stood on watch and didn't take care of himself. "Remember to eat."

"Yes, yes," he assured her in amusement.

"Stubborn man," she sighed, her last coherent thought. Then the world of dreams reached up and yanked her under.

Arandur watched her for a few moments: the peaceful expression on her face as sleep stole away her anxiety, the steady rise and fall of her chest as she breathed. Dark magic, but that had been terrifying. Bad enough for the problems with her senses to escalate, but what had cut him to the quick was seeing her obvious terror. Sevana had done her best to stay calm, to rationally report to him the problem, all the while sitting there like a child lost in a dark mountain. It had taken every ounce of control he had to not latch onto her.

But as much as he would have liked to say otherwise, his embrace was not a cure-all. Holding her would not fix the problem. He'd quickly fetched Ursilla for that reason, and was gratified when the woman immediately rolled out of her bed and came. Still, even with the expert calmly assuring them that this change was nothing to be alarmed about, Arandur prayed that nothing else like this would happen. He wasn't sure if his heart could take it, seeing that expression of dread on Sevana's face again.

Ursilla let out a gusty sigh that spoke volumes. "At the very least, can you not be so obvious in your affections, young man?"

Turning his head a few inches, Arandur regarded her steadily. Ursilla might have several hundred years on him, and she was a legend even among the Fae, but he felt no qualms in standing his ground. "Is there something wrong with one person loving another?"

She gave him the most maternal, exasperated look he'd ever received, and his own mother had been an expert at that look. "Your desire for her is not appropriate, Arandur."

"I do believe that's entirely between me and Sellion," he retorted mildly.

Pursing her lips, she stared at him through narrowed eyes. "Your ranking is beneath her. Such a union is not befitting of the Fae." When Arandur did not respond, she added, "You really think you can have her, don't you."

It was not a question. Arandur answered it anyway. "She told you before that she has argued with kings and won. She was not exaggerating. For that matter, she's argued with *gods* and won. Let's be clear on this, Ursilla. The only person whose opinion matters to me in this is Sellion's. When she chooses to give her heart, she will not seek approval from anyone else, least of all some antiquated custom. This is not a woman who can be dictated to."

Ursilla sat at the edge of the bed and watched him for a long, eternal moment. Then, strangely, she smiled. It was not a nice expression, but one that contained a great deal of challenge. "You think that by holding your ground like this, she'll eventually turn to you."

Arandur was not about to argue the point, or give voice to all the observations that he'd made over the past several months that gave him hope. He didn't want to explain that Sevana was a fiercely independent woman and that he'd watched her steadily include him into a very exclusive inner circle. He especially wouldn't tell her that the way Sevana now trusted him to be at her side, and the way she sometimes depended on him, was like an unspoken promise between them. The complexity of their relationship could not be summed up on paper, even if he used volumes in the attempt.

His silence, as it turned out, said quite a bit.

Shaking her head, Ursilla warned him, "Just by being with her, you won't win her heart. She's not one given to romance."

It took effort, but Arandur refrained from rolling his eyes at her and retorting with *'Tell me something I don't know.'* Arandur had no intention of just idly standing by and waiting for Sevana to notice. He just hadn't found the right timing yet. Not that he had any intention of telling Ursilla that, as that truly wasn't any of her business. As much as he appreciated the woman's magical help, he did not need her interference in his relationship with Sevana.

Something of that must have shown on his face, as Ursilla's brows quirked in challenge. "You're not one to be easily put off, I see. Just as well, if you're to have any chance of succeeding. I'll leave you to watch her. It goes without saying that you're to fetch me if you see anything strange."

"Of course," he agreed equably.

With a hum, she rose from the bed and drifted out again to her own guest quarters. Arandur tracked her with his ears more than his eyes. With her safely gone, Arandur fetched his bedding from the other room. If he were to be on vigil for the next several hours, there was no reason why he should be uncomfortable doing it. He fetched his journal while he was at it. Sevana had been making her own notes about the transformation process (as expected from one in her field), but her senses were still skewed, still human, and because of that, she missed a great deal. Arandur recorded everything he could observe with the hopes that when she was completely herself again, she could combine his observations with hers and leave an informative record for future generations.

Sevana didn't really know that he was doing this. Picturing her future response brought a smile on his face. She did love her data. Settling in a nest of blankets on the floor, he braced his back against the wall, the journal balanced on a knee. The smile lingered as he wrote, glancing up every page or so to check on her.

She'd be fine. They just had to weather the storm.

9

"I never thought I'd say this, but I'm glad to taste colors this morning," Sevana announced over breakfast. Well, somewhat breakfast. After being drugged to sleep eight hours solid, it was more like an early lunch. Words cannot express how relieved she was to wake up and have all of her senses functioning again. Perhaps not functioning correctly, but at least they were *working*. Sevana would take it as an improvement for now.

Aran had dark circles bruising under his eyes—the poor man really hadn't gotten much sleep in the past week because of her—but even so, he had a smile stretched from ear to ear. "You have no idea how happy I am about that too. Everything's still functioning?"

"Not correctly, but at least working," she confirmed, dashing salt along her shrimp. Sevana liked seafood fine, but she wasn't really accustomed to having it every meal. Khan did his best to supplement it by offering some land food, but apparently that was in short quantity down here, and he wasn't conversant enough with it to know what to buy. Having nothing but seafood and kelp, for days and at every meal, convinced her as nothing else had: she absolutely did not want to be Unda. Although it worried her that if she was already growing tired of fish at every meal now, only six days in, what would it be like in another five weeks? "In fact, I'm feeling well enough that I want to go out to the tubes today. I have a hunch."

Aran's hands paused as he dipped the shrimp into a small dish of sauce. "Another one?"

"Yes, well, I think this one will actually answer the question." Sevana'd had measured the tunnel for cracks. Not because she actually believed that air was seeping out—the pressure gauges at the engine station would have registered that problem—but because she had to rule it out as a possibility. The tubes were old, so ancient that no one in living memory remembered their construction, and among the Unda? Who could live hundreds of years? That was saying something.

Nothing built remained perfect, as time wore away at it. Especially underwater, as water was one of the most corrosive substances; it was natural for things to become porous over time. Even though Sevana didn't think that was the problem, she'd not been able to completely rule it out. It was a necessary first step to get the possibility out of the way, which Loman had done even while she'd been flat on her back, bless him.

Now, of course, she was well-rested, if not back to her normal self, and would much rather focus on theories than on the interesting twists and turns her body was undergoing.

Swallowing the bite in her mouth, she continued, "Remember the trouble we had with Nanashi Isle after the volcano blew? How the seafloor shifted and parts of it had moved, while other parts had tilted upwards?"

"Yes, certainly, it caused Nia Reign to nearly pull her hair out several times," Aran agreed, brows twisting upwards in confusion. "But we don't have a volcano here. Well, the ones at Kesly Isle, but they're too far away from here…" he trailed off, understanding slowly dawning over his face. "Kesly Station was the first to experience trouble."

"You're quick," she approved, waggling her eyebrows mischievously at him. "I'm not sure if this is part of Fae teaching, but you do know that the landmasses of the world are in a constant state of movement, right? It's ridiculously slow, takes centuries to even shift an inch, but they do move. With certain events—volcanoes, for example—the world experiences more dramatic shifts."

Aran leaned in, his breakfast completely forgotten. "But the Kesly Isles are in a constant state of eruption. You told me that at Nanashi."

"I was not wrong. They *are* in a constant state of eruption. But that just adds fuel to my theory." Her hands rose to illustrate her point, gesturing to the world beyond their breakfast table. "Think of it this way. If something had happened—an earthquake, for instance—it wouldn't have been a burning question, would it? After the system became unusable, someone would have linked the two together and come to the right hypothesis. They would have *expected* the earthquake to have something to do with it. But the Kesly volcanoes? Those have been going off for eighty years, at least, why think of them? But that's the very reason I suspect them. They're steadily releasing pressure on a daily basis."

"And slowly changing the movements of the seafloor in the process," Arandur finished slowly, tone ruminative. "You think that's what happened. The tubes are out of joint?"

"At least some of them. Why would a passenger pod be merrily blazing along its intended tube, only to be sucked into a branch tube? Either it was forcefully drawn there, or the slope of the tube was such that it tipped it over. The passengers would have felt it if it was something forceful. My bet's on the latter."

"How do you even begin to prove that? Is there a way to measure the slope?"

"Sure. I can't use my tools, but I guarantee Loman has some that will do the trick. The question that I'm still puzzled over," she reached for her water glass idly, "is why the pods are getting stuck mid-tunnel. Nothing has given me any clues on that. Every test we ran that first day came back normal."

Arandur shook his head in fond amusement as he returned to his breakfast. "You say that but you're practically bouncing in your chair. You don't want to fix this problem quickly."

"And leave me bored while stuck down here for another five weeks? Of course I don't." Sevana thought that rather obvious, really. Right now, she could only theoretically solve the problem. She couldn't actually apply her magic or skills to physically put that fix into practice. It was perhaps not nice of her, to want to delay solving the riddle, but when was she ever nice?

"Would the slope change the tunnels enough to explain why the pods get stuck sometimes?"

"Sure, but only with a dramatic shift. If it goes down a foot, or up a foot, it would be enough to cause problems. But I think someone would have noticed that by now, wouldn't you? They've walked the tunnels multiple times, and anything that obvious would have been pointed out." Shaking her head, she went back to her shrimp porridge. "No, this is something very subtle, something that the naked eye alone cannot perceive. Which is why you need to hurry and eat, there's a lot of measuring I need to do."

"Do I get a nap today?" he asked drily, as if fully prepared for the answer to be 'no.'

"Certainly, I won't stop you." With mock sweetness she gestured to his cot. "You can stay here and nap while I go."

"You know very well that I will never, in a hundred years, leave your side when you're in a vulnerable state."

"Yup." Sevana nodded, not even bothering to tamp down her smirk. "Which was why I didn't suggest it."

Shaking his head, he went back to eating.

Aran really was setting himself up for this, in her opinion. It was his fault that he liked her so much that he was willing to stay up all night and tramp after her today. Sevana, perhaps, should have made allowances, but in truth she had no idea how long it would take for her to solve this problem, and the idea of being stuck under the sea past her transformation? Completely shudder-worthy. Arandur likely agreed with her on this point, hence why he didn't try to slow her down where work was concerned. Better to have the problem solved before it was time for her to leave than the reverse.

Besides, she still had to gather materials for Sarsen and Master, and that list was hefty enough that it couldn't possibly be done in a single day. She needed to allot time for that as well. It was actually quite a bit of work to shoehorn into five weeks' time, if one factored in her questionable health and energy levels.

They pulled on shoes and left shortly after that, walking the streets toward the station. Of course, luck dictated that they only get some dozen paces from the house before being accosted by Rane.

The queen had her dark hair piled up on her head in an elaborate coiffure of combs and pearls, her slender form moving fluidly in a dark blue dress that looked like the deepest sections of the ocean, which set off her pale skin. An effect she obviously knew to be pretty, judging from that regal tilt of her head. Anyone who passed by her gave a bow automatically, then whispered to each other on how lively their queen looked today.

Sevana could only take so much of the woman's internal preening before cutting it short. "Rane. I suppose you're here for an update."

"I wanted to see how you were doing, too," she responded with an open pout, as if this statement was somehow an accusation against her empathy.

"I thought Kira was keeping an eye on me and giving updates?"

Soundly ignoring that, Rane made a show of looking her up and down. "You're certainly changing quickly, much faster than our children do. Ursilla thinks this wise?"

"A more gradual transformation would actually be harder on me, as it gives my magical core more wiggle room to battle things out," Sevana explained, not entirely patiently. "And a decade of this would drive me and everyone around me mad."

"Ah. A point I should have considered." No skin off her nose, Rane waved this away as inconsequential. "I will walk with you as you tell me what progress you've made."

In order to better show off to her subjects? Sevana heaved a gusty sigh and resigned herself to a pointless few minutes of conversation. Setting off at a ground-eating stride, she tried to make this a shining example of brevity. "In short, I have eliminated what it cannot be."

Rane turned her head just so in order to frown down at the shorter woman. "Loman reported to me that you have only been at the station once. You determined all of that in a day?"

"Not really. I mean, Loman and his crew have been testing every possible way for years, all I had to do was ask what they'd tried. Loman ran a few tests for me so I could see the results myself and get a better feel for matters. But basically, we've ruled out the possibilities." Sevana ticked them off on her fingers. "Your station engine is working fine. The tubes are holding pressure fine. There's nothing wrong with the pods. All of this is important information for us, as we can focus on what's remaining."

"Indeed?" Rane's expression said quite clearly that she had no idea what could possibly be remaining.

Loathe as she was to repeat herself, Sevana found herself doing just that and relating exactly what she'd just told Aran over breakfast. This task was particularly odorous, as Aran had moved to walk behind her when Rane joined them. It made sense for him to show decorous behavior with the queen of Living Waters, but in Sevana's eyes he was every bit on her level. And she was getting increasingly irritated that no one else shared that opinion.

What was *wrong* with these people? The Fae had levels of formality and different ranks, but they also didn't hang every decision on it. Aran could go directly to Aranhil and speak with him if he wanted to. If he tried something similar with the Unda, they'd be horrified. Despite being cousin races, they were clearly different when it came to protocol.

Not for the first time, Sevana patted herself on the back for a decision well made. She would have gone mad if she were Unda.

Because of her peregrinations she missed the first half of Rane's question.

"—not seen any difference anywhere else, so how can you be sure?" Rane's face scrunched up in a doubtful frown.

Inferring what she'd missed, Sevana stated confidently, "I'm not sure. That's why we're measuring things this morning. Frankly, it's the only thing that makes sense to me, though. A subtle enough rise or tilt of the sea floor would do this, I believe, and it wouldn't be obvious to an observer."

"So if this isn't the problem?" Rane challenged.

Shrugging, Sevana admitted, "I go back to the drawing board. Granted, I don't think this is the reason for both problems. I'm just reasonably sure that it's the cause for the pods that are sometimes sucked into different tunnels. I need detailed specifications and blueprints of the tunnels, measurements, and more time to figure out why the pods get stuck halfway to their destination. I know it's not a pressure problem, but that's all I can say for sure at this point."

That did not satisfy Rane but she nodded, accepting it. "Keep me updated. I want to know what progress you make. If you wish to go to our sister clan and test their engines, inform me of that as well. I will send an escort with you."

"I will," Sevana promised. So she didn't have to ask for that? Good. It saved her a little trouble. "In fact, I likely will need to. They experienced trouble first, but that doesn't mean they have the same problem that we do. It could be coincidence that both stations developed problems one right after the other. It could be it's interconnected. I won't know until I take a look."

"I understand." Rane let out a gusty sigh. "I'd hoped for a quick resolution, but I suppose that was naïve of me. You're not at your best, after all."

"That will slow me down," Sevana agreed with saccharine sweetness.

Hearing the acid in her tone, Rane waved her down impatiently. "Oh stop, Sellion. I don't mean it that way. We're all very excited to be able to travel again, is all. We all have perfect faith that you'll manage to solve it. It's just, well, we're all tired of braving the waters and swimming for long distances to reach our destinations. You can understand, I'm sure."

Considering Sevana had multiple vehicles to help her reach destinations more quickly, she could completely sympathize. "I can only work so fast, so be patient. My senses are not trustworthy at the moment, but that's part of why Aran is with me."

"Yes, in regards to that." Rane paused at the crossroads and half-turned to regard Aran. Her opinion was scrawled all over her face. "I believe that I can appoint others who are more beneficial to you."

Sevana's mouth opened on a hot retort, because queen or not, Rane had just crossed an unforgiveable line.

She never got a syllable out before Aran was right in the queen's face, staring her down. "There is no one who understands her methods or needs more than me. I will not leave her side."

"You are here to help her rebirth," Rane argued coolly. "Do not think that gives you the right to determine your place here."

"I am here because Aranhil appointed me here," Aran riposted, each word clipped and blunt. "I am here because Sellion requested it. I am not here at your sufferance, nor under your authority."

Rane's eyebrows shot straight up into her hairline in surprise. The whole scene froze, as the pedestrians around them caught part of the exchange and stared at Aran as if he were begging for his head to get chopped off. Rane's mouth dropped in shock before she snapped it closed again. Sevana nearly said something, but paused and waited to see how Rane would respond first.

To everyone's surprise, Rane's mouth stretched into a shark-like grin, her head tipping as she gave Aran a look, like a bomb politely asking if it could join the party and blow everything to kingdom come. "I'd wondered at the quality of the man at Sellion's side. She is not one to suffer fools, after all, but you follow her lead so amiably I took you as one."

Aran quirked a brow at her, just the slightest arch, and returned her stare levelly.

"I am glad to be mistaken." True amusement finally sparked in her eyes and she gave him the slightest dip of the chin, a silent approval. "You have my permission to stay with her, Arandur of South Woods, whether you require it or not. Sellion, keep me informed."

With that, Rane drifted off, continuing her own way.

The curious onlookers were slower to disburse. Sevana watched Aran's face, saw the way his jaw clenched, his hands flexing into almost fists at his side. Had he, too, hit his limit with how he was treated down here? No, that didn't seem quite right. He'd known before coming, had accepted it, and Aran's patience was nearly limitless. Something else was going on here.

"Do I need to apologize?" he asked her quietly, still staring after Rane's retreating back.

The question didn't make sense to Sevana for a moment. Apologize for what, standing up for himself? Sevana was frankly relieved he'd finally done so, surely he knew that. It took a moment for the obvious to dawn on her. It wasn't that—Aran had no care for what Rane thought of him—rather, he was asking if Sevana thought his behavior inappropriate (yes, but Sevana adored inappropriate), or something that she would later regret (no, never).

Delighted, Sevana linked her arm with his and pulled him along. "The next person who challenges you, smack 'em. I have no patience with this nonsense. If I had a problem with you, that would be between me and you. Not them."

"Even if it's the Queen of Living Waters?" Relieved, he matched her stride, eyes soft with affection as he watched her.

Sevana grinned in a way that never spoke well for innocent bystanders. "Especially if it's her."

"Why do I have to be the responsible one?" Aran sighed to himself, acting put upon. She could tell that he was secretly delighted, though. "We don't want to start an international incident, remember? Aren't you going to be good?"

"I'm going to be me."

"Uh-oh." His worried look needed more work. Aran's evil delight seeped through.

Cackling, a skip in her step, Sevana shooed off any thoughts of diplomacy. She had Aran and a puzzle to solve. That took priority over everything else.

10

Sevana's good humor survived approximately three hours before frustration reared its ugly head. She'd gone over every inch of the tunnel, the one that caused the most trouble when it came to shooting passengers down the wrong line. If there was a sloping issue here, it was impossible to tell from the inside.

The build of each tunnel was perfectly circular, the walls smooth to the touch in order to speed along the pods. Standing in the center of it, several hundred paces inside, she glared toward the darker section ahead. Only a lamp (or what passed for a lamp down here; it was actually a sea sparkle plankton captured in a glass tube) in her hand illuminated the area, and she growled toward the man standing behind her, "I don't like this tunnel. It refuses to give up its secrets."

"You want to go outside and do measurements, don't you?" Aran's tone made it less of a question than a statement.

"There's no point trying to do this from the inside," she argued, turning sharply on her heel. "The slope is too gradual; we literally cannot detect it within this space. I need something longer than twelve feet."

He grimaced, but it was more in resignation than protest. Sevana knew they were due to be back for another treatment in four hours, and that this job would likely take more than four hours to complete if they had to walk out along the sea floor. But he also understood after watching her work that sometimes just facts and figures weren't enough. To really grasp the situation properly, it was best if she could see it with her own eyes.

"I don't wish to delay your treatments," Aran stated slowly, gauging her reaction with every syllable out of his mouth.

Sevana appreciated that he was trying not to start an argument even as he put his own opinion out into the air. "I understand that. I don't want to either. I don't think I need to be out there for long. What I need is an answer for this particular tunnel. If I'm right, we can measure all of the others and get a better understanding for how the slope has changed. If I'm wrong, then I know to toss this theory."

Relieved, he gave her a nod. "Alright. That's sensible. Let's go see if there's any truth to this idea, then."

Sevana had not wanted to go out without him, although she would have if he'd dug his heels in. This way was much better, as it meant less friction between them. Happy, she stretched her legs out in a speed walk, calling ahead of her as she moved, "LOMAN!"

A shadowy figure appeared at the end of the tunnel. "Yes, Artifactor?"

Strange how she was someone specific to different people. They each had their way of calling her, depending on the role she inhabited in their lives. Shaking off the thought, she focused. "Loman, I think we need to go outside and measure this."

Loman's head bobbed up and down, agreeing. "Yes, I think we can't conclude anything from the measurements in here. I had Pol go and collect the surveyors. They'll meet us outside."

She really did like Loman. The man was quick on the uptake and not concerned about waiting hand and foot on her. It moved things along nicely. She reached him, but he was already half-turned, body language impatient to step out of their air bubble in this area and into the sea beyond the invisible walls. Assuming he would escort her outside himself, she fell into step with him, not surprised when Loman erected a barrier around the three of them so that they could continue to breathe.

Sevana had done this several times before, just stepping outside into the cool ocean water as if she had gills. Her body, however, was sharply aware that it did not have gills and the weight of the water above her head could crush her if she were unwary. Her survival instincts flinched as she stepped outside and it took extreme effort to keep panic at bay. Surely, after all of her experience, this should get easier?

Neither Loman or Arandur seemed to notice her reaction, and Sevana kept it carefully out of her body language and off her face as they proceeded forward. The rocks under her boots shifted, slick and wet, but they were in no hurry and didn't try to jog. The exterior of the tubes were covered in thick meadows of Posidonia, the plants green, thin and blade-like. That intrigued Sevana, as she was sure that the plant could only survive at a specific depth under the ocean's surface, as it had to have good light penetration to survive, and would die off if the water was too cloudy.

"Loman. For the record, how far down are we?"

"At this juncture?" Loman paused and looked around him. "I would say, perhaps a hundred and twenty feet?"

"Are all of the tunnels at that depth?"

"No, no, of course not. That varies depending on where the tunnels are. It's why we can only go from station to station."

Sevana nodded in understanding. The vacuum pull worked very well, of course, but it would be considerably slowed if the tunnel had large variations along the route. Too many ups and downs, curves, or slopes would disrupt it and make the interruption of the pods' progress more statistically likely. Breaking it up between stations to make sure that the tunnels stayed as level and true as possible only made sense. "The builders of the system knew what they were doing."

"Our history actually says it took much trial and error. Their first system was that of water pressure instead of air vacuum." Loman cast her a wry smile.

Picturing this, Sevana snickered, not in sympathy for those ancient engineers. "How badly did that go?"

"Quite badly," Loman answered blandly.

That might well be the understatement of the century. She almost asked another question, but movement out of the corner of her eye snagged her attention instead. Glancing over, she found that a team of mermen swam rapidly in their direction. Loman waved in greeting, then let out a sonorous sound like something a whale would utter. Hearing that deep call echo out of this man's average body startled her. Sevana knew that the Fae could speak to any animal, that was common knowledge, but actually witnessing an Unda use that ability to speak to his comrades through the water was fascinating all the same.

That long, mournful sound seemed to be sufficient instruction, as the four-man team nodded understanding before two swam in one direction, the others going opposite. Each of them carried something that looked remarkably like a sextant in their hands, and at a certain point, the other two swam away from their partners. It took a moment for Sevana to figure out exactly what they were doing.

"Are we the benchmark?" she inquired of Loman.

"Indeed."

She chose to stay quiet as everyone spread out in their various positions. If they were the 'level' then everything would be measured against them and Loman would need to focus. With his hands full, she pulled out the miniature journal from her bag and wrote down the columns for back-sight, height of instrument, foresight, elevation and description. The other side of the page she left blank and ready for the equations.

"Run one hundred feet," Loman informed her without taking his eyes away from the sextant in his hands.

Sevana scribbled that down and was grateful for the distance. An even number like this made the calculations that much easier. The surveyors had likely done this on purpose.

"Rise…" A frown gathered over Loman's face, layer upon layer, signally his suspicions. "Rise is forty-eight."

Making a note, she studied his expression from the corner of her eye. "What was it before?"

"Fifty-two," he answered slowly. "Or very close to fifty-two. It seems you might be on to something, Artifactor."

Two of the other surveyors had been making their own measurements and they called out the number to Loman in that whale-like sound. It gave her eerie chills racing up and down her spine, but in a good sense, as if something just outside her understanding wrapped around her.

"Run of one hundred, rise of fifty," Loman translated for her.

Aran leaned his head over her shoulder and watched as she did quick calculations and graphed the slope. "In other words, you have a two percent slope going down, and a one percent slope going across?"

Letting out a sound that might have been a garbled curse, Loman stared hard at the land before letting his sextant drop. "Artifactor. I think I owe you an apology."

She grinned without looking up from her journal. "Your toes were stepped on and feelings hurt when Rane called me in. I knew that. Understandable, really. I'd be the same in your shoes. But Loman, she called me in for fresh eyes and because I can think outside the box."

"She called you in because you can figure out the problem," Loman corrected wearily. Still, when she glanced up, he looked relieved instead of angry, his shoulders unwinding from the clench he'd been holding around her. "I don't mind, as long as I can finally fix this. You think the slope caused all of this?"

"I think the slope is the reason the pods sometimes go into the wrong tunnel branches," she corrected. "Intersecting tunnels would be tipped just enough to cause the pods to turn into them. The reason why they stop midway still puzzles me. I don't need to tell you how to fix this, do I?"

With a shake of the head, he wet his lips with a light of determination in his eyes. "No. We'll manage that just fine. You've another treatment today, haven't you?"

"Yes, and it will likely knock me flat on my back for at least tomorrow. At least, everything else has basically done so. You work on correcting the slopes, then contact your sister stations and have them make the same measurements, see if it's a similar problem between all the stations."

Loman likely didn't need the order but he nodded along anyway. "I'll lay odds it is."

"So will I, but I try not to make assumptions. They tend to

come back and punch me in the face. Hardly pleasant." Closing the journal, she replaced it in her bag before slinging it around to rest against her lower back. "And I want this confirmed. As for the other problem…give me the measurements and the construction blueprints for this station's tunnels. I'll study them if I can tomorrow and maybe something will leap out at me."

"Loman, can you send us back now?" Aran requested with an apologetic splay of the hands. "We need to head in."

"Yes, of course, I'll call Pol over." Loman this time used a sharp series of barks, not at all unlike what a seal would use.

Sevana had to assume that he switched animal languages as he did because one of the languages performed the nuances better than another. Perhaps once she was fully Fae, she'd understand precisely why he chose the animals he did and exactly what he was saying. It couldn't simply be an Unda thing, as Aran clearly had no trouble following what everyone was saying.

As they waited for Pol to swim the short distance to them, Loman fixed her with a very firm look. She knew that look well, as Master aimed it at her on a regular basis. It was part suspicion, part paternal, with a glimmer of an idea lurking in between the two. "You've really no idea why the pods stop at the reef?"

"You really think that kind of gradual slope is going to be enough to stop a hi-velocity pod in its tracks?" she shot back, knowing very well what it was that he suspected. "It's a two percent slope, man! Of course it's not going to stop a pod dead. It might, if it were a more severe drop, slow it within a hundred feet, but this is more like twenty. That's insane—nothing should have that stopping force. Something's impeding the pods. We just have to determine what."

Sighing, he went back to staring at the tunnel in visible frustration.

"Loman, we will figure this out," Sevana promised him, meaning every word. "In the meantime, fix those slopes and report to Rane and Curano what we've discovered here today. Progress will make them happy."

Peering at her under his eyebrows, Loman's suspicious look shifted. "Why don't you report that to them?"

"I've had enough of people for today." Sevana was only half-joking. Mostly, she was half-serious. Encountering Rane once a day was her limit, thank you very much. Something about that woman drove her up the wall.

Pol arrived and stepped into the air bubble, making it rather crowded. Loman didn't seem convinced that she really did not want to talk to royalty, but shrugged and let it go, stepping out to give Pol room and control. The assistant was a sprightly young thing, on the thin side with hair perpetually in his eyes. If he was older than fifty, Sevana would eat her boots. He was barely adult compared to Fae standards. With a deferential duck of the head to her and Arandur, he started their trek back into the main city.

Keeping pace easily, Sevana mused, "Although, really, I wonder why the pods stop. I keep saying that the pressure gauges don't see a drop in vacuum in the tunnels, but perhaps something's interfering with the instruments?"

Over his shoulder, Pol spoke in a soft voice, almost timid. "We did check that, Artifactor."

"Curses, of course you did." Pursing her lips together, Sevana tried to think of other possibilities. Nothing, unfortunately, sprang to mind. "I really don't think it's the slope, but I suppose if you can fix one of the tunnels and try sending a pod through, it'll tell us clearly or not if the problem still exists. Who knows, I might turn out wrong."

Aran mock gasped, putting a palm to his chest. "You? Wrong?"

Just for that, she smacked him with the back of her hand against his side. He snickered, not at all bothered by it. Really, the man could be such a brat. It's probably why they were able to be friends. Nice people didn't last long around Sevana.

With no immediate answer on hand, Sevana's mind switched to what would come next: her daily dose of Fae blood. Ursilla had made no mention of what she wanted to tackle next, which made Sevana wonder aloud, "What do you think Ursilla will choose to focus on this time? Senses? It would be nice if those straightened themselves out."

Aran's silence was eloquent.

Her eyes shot up to his. "Not my magical core again."

"Oh, no, I didn't think that. But you do have other body parts, you realize? And in order for your senses to adapt fully, we'll need to physically change your organs at some point." A grimace of anticipation on his face, he admitted morosely, "Although I know it's not going to be pleasant for you, it'll be better to get it over with."

That was a fact. The dread of the thing was often worse than the thing itself, after all. Half-resigned already, Sevana observed rhetorically, "If you're right, and you likely are, it's just as well Loman won't need me for the next several days. I'll definitely be flat on my back if she goes for my eyes, or something like that."

"Truly. But once you're completely changed, you'll stop having magical accidents, and won't that make this all worth it?"

Sevana grunted sourly. "That does sound good, don't get me wrong, but you might have to keep reminding me of it. I'm likely to forget when I'm writhing about on the bed like a landed fish."

He slid an arm around her shoulders and hugged her to his side for a moment. "It will be fine, Sevana."

11

It was fine. Well, that was to say, Sevana didn't feel like she was either going to implode, explode, or became a gelatin goo by the evening. That said, she didn't feel up to traipsing about outside either. Her sense of touch was finally straightened out, as was taste, but sight seemed on the fritz. Not that she mentioned that to either Aran or Ursilla. Instead of tasting colors, she now either saw everything in shades of purple—why purple?—or it turned grayscale. The switch back and forth came without any warning whatsoever, and Sevana did not think it wise to try and work outside with her vision this unstable.

But sitting here at the table with the blueprints of the tunnels and the schematics for the engines, as well as the logs of what natural disasters had occurred in the past fifty years, was something still well within her ability. It might also hold the key to what was actually going wrong down here, more than skulking along the tubes would do.

Volcanoes always erupted down here, of course—not in this precise region, but in the neighboring area of Kesly Isles. That could be a contributing factor. The logs mentioned a few minor earthquakes, more felt as a rumble than anything, barely hard enough to rattle the dishes and knock pictures askew. This area had experienced two in the past thirty years, and Sevana's eyes narrowed as she read the entries, her finger skimming along the page as she read the rather spidery handwriting. Minor earthquakes. Not an uncommon thing around the seafloor, certainly, which was likely why no one thought anything of them. Certainly they hadn't remembered them or mentioned them to her, but this might answer her questions. Or at least give her a good culprit to point to. Why had the tunnels suddenly developed a two percent slope downhill?

Because the earth had shifted in the earthquakes. Simple.

The front door opened as Aran returned from his errand. Sevana had heard him say something, although she hadn't been paying close enough attention to remember why he'd gone out. He'd rarely left her side since coming down here, so even if it had just been an excuse to take a breather from her, she wouldn't have blamed him. Certainly just watching her pour over schematics and history logs couldn't be riveting.

He shucked off his boots at the door and said something to her, and she hummed back a response, her eyes still mostly focused on the documents. That last earthquake was more intense than the first one. It'd happened nearly ten years ago now, so Sevana could hardly call it recent. But something about the date of the occurrence bothered her. That date was familiar—or at least, it connected to some other fact she'd heard, although she couldn't immediately put a finger on it.

Aran was still saying something, but she barely caught a word of it. He sounded serious, and the way his words lilted up at the end invited a response of some sort.

When the silence stretched for more than a second, she lifted her eyes up to his. Whatever he'd been saying, his expression looked hopeful, as if he wished for her to agree. Since she likely owed him several favors at this juncture, Sevana had no problem with doing whatever he had in mind. "Yes, alright."

A wide smile took over his face, his entire demeanor lighting up with so much joy he looked nearly incandescent with it. Oh dear, what had she just agreed to?

Without a single word to her, he crossed the distance between them in two large strides, caught her face with both hands in a gentle caress, and leaned down to softly, insistently kiss her.

Sevana blinked in surprise. She'd never been kissed in her life. As startled as she was, she had to admit the bards who sang all of those love songs might be onto something after all. Kissing was actually quite pleasant. Not that she had any idea what had pleased Aran so much that he'd kissed her to show his appreciation, but she wasn't about to dissuade him. She lifted up a little more, her hands coming up to rest against his chest as she attempted to kiss back.

That pleased him; he smiled for a moment and gave a contented hum. Gently disengaging, he gave her a warm hug, lingering. "Thank you. I know I interrupted you, I'll let you get back to your research, but let's take proper time for dinner, alright?"

"Sure," she agreed, still bewildered on what she'd agreed to. After he left, Sevana sat in the chair and picked things back up again, but eventually stared uselessly at them. What had that been all about? It had felt very nice, and she wouldn't mind doing it again, but why?

Sevana felt like someone had unexpectedly tilted the world on her. She'd never thought of Aran in a romantic vein before. Scratch that—she'd never thought of romance at all. With that kiss, he'd opened a door where she hadn't expected to find one, and the view on the other side of it was enticing indeed.

What would it be like, she wondered, to have Aran as a life partner? A friend, a lover, a spouse, all rolled into one? Did she want that? Her mind flashed back to the kiss, unbidden, and her lips tingled, heartbeat speeding up a touch. Alright, that was possibly a stupid question. Clearly she did want that. It took more than a few minutes to mentally adjust to this possibility. The more she thought on it, the more perks she found, and few things to object to.

Aran as a romantic partner. Maybe she needed to explore this possibility further.

After the kiss came a host of casual touches when in their guest house. Though he did not attempt to kiss her again, Aran was not shy about hugging her good morning, or brushing a hand along her shoulders when passing behind her, or nudging her with a hip and ordering her to stop hogging the couch. Apparently, he also saw no reason to observe arbitrary personal boundaries in private.

Sevana startled at first, as she couldn't understand why he was suddenly acting outside of his norm, but she really couldn't say that she minded. It was strange, to have him suddenly inside of her personal space more often than not, and behaving so affectionately with her, but Sevana couldn't deny that she liked it. Certainly it helped her realize that exploring something romantic with him was a very agreeable idea.

It also made focusing on the problem at hand more difficult, as Sevana's long-dormant interest in things outside of academia suddenly reared its head. Between that and the next two treatments from Aran, she couldn't seem to focus on work for more than a handful of hours a day. Really, it was appalling. And if Kip, Sarsen, or Master had been around to see this, they would have laughed their fool heads off and thrown out a few (admittedly justified) I-told-you-so's.

But even with all of the interruptions to her work, Sevana did not want Aran to retreat again to a respectable distance. She had no idea what had brought this on, and for once, she wished she'd actually been paying attention to the conversation. Aran had clearly asked her something important, but short of owning up to the matter—and she'd rather have needles shoved under her nails—she couldn't admit that she'd not been paying attention. After that first day, he hadn't kissed her again, although he often dropped a kiss on her forehead or her cheek. And hugs occurred far more frequently than usual.

Perhaps he'd just been very happy that first day? Because of whatever-she'd-agreed-to? It didn't entirely make sense to her, but relationships in general didn't make much sense to her. Really, in her opinion, people were just balls of emotions and energy. It's why Sevana found them to be generally exhausting.

Aran had always been affectionate with her, not like the way Master or Sarsen was, but more…something. She had a hard time defining it, even in her head, but he acted different now. In fact, now that she thought about it, he sometimes did things or said something similar to how Bel reacted around Hana. Strange thought, as Sevana had never put the concept of romance and herself in the same circle, and yet the idea lingered. Lingered quite pleasantly, truth be told. Sevana's interest in all things romantic couldn't be used to fill up a thimble, but a woman would have to be rotting in the grave to not see Aran's appeal.

As a teenager, Sevana had put aside any fanciful notions of true love or romance because, truthfully, just friendships were hard for her to maintain. The past year had been the hardest of her life, and yet Aran had stuck through it with her. That was clearly a good indication of her changes with him, and Sevana was of the opinion that perhaps, just perhaps, if for once in her life she wasn't too disagreeable, she could persuade Aran to become something more than a friend.

Yes, it sounded like wishful thinking, even in her own head, but Sevana still determined to have a go at it.

And she might be rubbish at relationships, but she did understand that going out and doing fun things was a necessary part of showing your interest in someone. With four weeks to go until she became Fae, Sevana wasn't physically up to much, but she did manage to come up with something.

Over breakfast that morning, she inquired casually, "Do you want to do a bit of shopping this morning?"

Aran's spoon paused halfway to his mouth. "Shopping? Do you need something?"

"I still have a list of things for Master and Sarsen," she reminded him, idly twisting her water glass without truly picking it up from the table. "I believe I can get most of it from the local market, but likely not all. Loman and his engineers are still measuring the lines of the tubes and adjusting slopes, so there's not much I can do today, work-wise. I can't run any tests until they're done. So, shopping?"

His face relaxed into a smile. "A day to unwind sounds brilliant to me. Although the way you said that worries me. Just what are we looking for?"

Sevana had the list memorized and rattled it off, ticking items on her fingers as she went. "Sirens' song, conch shells larger than my hand, kraken ink, any sea gems uncut, any fins from sea serpents, aspidochelone turtle shells, and a dozen uncarved sea stones."

Aran's eyebrows had lifted at the start of this list and gradually climbed at her recitation until they were lodged into his hairline. "I know you said earlier that you didn't think you could collect all of that in a day. I now understand why. At least half of that list is likely not going to be found in a marketplace, not even an Unda marketplace."

"Uncut sea gems, conch shells, kraken ink, and the uncarved sea stones I'm reasonably sure that I can buy. The rest of it…" she trailed off, flipping her hand over in a shrug. "We'll see. I'm not in a fit state to go hunting for things myself, even if I could breathe comfortably underwater, which means we need to find a merchant who can track things down for me. And I need to give him time to do that. So, shopping today would be best."

"I'm all for it. But do you have the energy?"

"I feel fine at the moment." Wryly, she tacked on, "Let's capitalize on it."

They did, and not entirely the way that Sevana expected. She'd made it a whole three feet from the guest house when Aran took her hand and placed it in the crook of his elbow, as if escorting her. But it didn't feel anything so formal. This was part of that affection from the past several days, and she encouraged it by walking a little closer to him than normal, which put a smile on his face. Huh. Perhaps she was terrible with romancing men, but she knew Aran well enough to read him. At least she had that going for her.

The market for Living Waters was a bustling, thriving area that took up three streets and could put any capital's main market to shame. The streets weren't any wider here than they had been in the neighborhood, but the stores were crammed in side-by-side without even the possibility of slipping a sheet of paper between them. People crammed in as well, jostling Sevana and Aran on both sides. It was quite an eclectic collection, Unda in both their human and selkie forms, and Sevana received more than one curious look from those who had the eyes to see her semi-transformed state. Sevana ignored those soundly.

Fortunately, the market resided under the air barrier, which Sevana felt grateful for, as navigating it would have been tricky otherwise.

Since Aran had a good head of height on her, she asked him, "Do you see anything on our list?"

"Conch shells, dead ahead and to the right. Who designed these streets, anyway? Even I could get lost down here."

Snorting at the near whine in his voice, she admitted, "They are as twisty as the wrinkles on a crone's face, I do admit. But I have complete faith you won't get us lost."

"Is that…" he glanced down at her, making a show of being perplexed, although his twitching lips spoiled the effect, "is that a challenge? Or a threat?"

Patting his chest, she batted her eyes at him. "Yes."

"There are days I think you deliberately confuse me. Just for the cheap entertainment value." Shaking his head, he shifted to block the traffic heading toward them, just long enough for both of them to squeeze through, gaining the long counter booth under the striped yellow and green awning overhead. Sevana nearly tripped over someone's foot and had to scramble a mite to keep her feet and balance. Her hold on Aran's arm saved her in the end, and she didn't miss the sharp look he gave her, as if unsure if her vertigo had decided to come back for another round.

Waving him down—she was fine, it was just crowded here—she focused on the wares. The scent of the sea was stronger here, a fierce mix of brine, water, and that mystical odor of the ocean that escaped description. The conch shells were plentiful on this side of the table, a light yellow on the outside, the insides a pearly white deepening to a hot pink inside the shell. Some of them were white and beige in color, others grey with a green interior, still others with a striation of tan and orangey-red around the outside. Quite a respectable mix, really.

Trouble was, half of them were completely unsuitable. Lifting her head, she caught the shopkeeper's eye, a lumbering seal that chose not to be in his human form today. He had a monocle perched on his right eye and a money bag hanging about his neck from a golden chord. "Master. Have you any conchs grown from the sea?"

"My dear customer, they are all grown from the sea," he returned in a chittering voice, amused.

Praying for patience, she negated, "These are all raised. I mean wild conchs, not harvested."

His head lifted, body language indicating interest. "You can tell in a glance?"

Aran gestured toward her with a hand, still standing protectively at her side to protect her from the jostling pedestrians passing them by, "This esteemed lady is Artifactor Sevana Warren."

"Ahh, my thanks, Artifactor, for visiting my humble shop. I do have a selection of native conchs in the back. They are not normally as popular, you see, as they're rather plain in appearance."

"I need them for their power, not their looks," Sevana explained patiently. "Have you anything larger than my spread hand?" She held it up in illustration.

The shopkeeper's head bobbed up and down. "Yes, yes, quite a few. Mila! Fetch the red box!"

Someone behind the green-and-yellow striped curtain let out a muffled yip that sounded like acceptance of the order, then came the rustle of boxes being shifted, barely heard over the shuffle of the crowd behind and around Sevana. It took a moment, but eventually a woman with clear skin and large, round eyes appeared with a flat, red box in her hands. She carefully levered it so that the edge rested on the table's surface and she could tilt it forward, allowing Sevana a good look at the wares inside.

In a bed of shredded paper sat perhaps a dozen conch shells, each of them a variety of colors and sizes, but all of them the size of her hand. Two were substantially larger. Even at a glance, Sevana could see the power of them and gave a satisfied grunt. "Yes, that's more like it. Master, how much for the box?"

He named a price that made her grimace. Seriously, if she didn't owe Master and Sarsen such a huge favor, she'd consider these souvenirs of theirs to be highway robbery. "I'm also looking for untouched sea stones and uncut gems. Do you have anything along those lines?"

"I don't," he denied thoughtfully, his round dark eyes shrewd, "but my brother does. Two shops down. He's new to business, just starting out. If you'll go and buy something from him, I'll have these wrapped and taken to your guest house free of charge."

That was something, at least. "I'll do that."

Aran's head swiveled as he tried to ascertain which shop exactly. "The other awning that also has green and yellow stripes is his?"

"The very one, Master Fae."

With a wince on her face, Sevana paid out, although if this trend kept up, it would be a very short shopping trip. Master would have to send her funds or she'd have to go and collect things herself somehow because there was no way she could pay for all of this with what she had on her. Where was Kip when she needed him? He could have bought all of this and probably a few services to boot with what she had in her purse.

The stop at the next shop went a little better, as she got the sea stones at a reasonable price, bartering in turn that she sign a letter of authentication for the rest of the inventory. Sevana happily did so, as it was in fact good quality stock, and it saved her a ridiculous amount of money.

Aran stayed right by her side, sometimes pressing in closer as he was jostled from behind, which left her more physically aware of him than usual. Had he really always been this much taller? This broad in the chest? Sevana knew him to be strong, but the way he half-lifted her with one arm to shift her abruptly out of the way of a reckless drunk startled her. Sevana knew him well, or thought she did, but suddenly she questioned her observational powers. Why did she feel she was only now properly seeing him?

Despite the crowded conditions of the market, and the stress of watching her money slowly slip through her fingers, Sevana actually enjoyed the outing. Most of that was due to Aran, who wasn't a demanding shopping companion, and surprised her a time or two by ducking down and whispering a hilarious observation into her ear. Sevana tired faster than she liked, and they paused in the international district to have something not-sea food related for a snack.

Sitting at the small, round table with the waffle cone in her hand, she moaned in bliss. "Never have strawberries and waffles tasted so excellent."

"It's just as well that you didn't choose to become Unda," Aran remarked idly, licking a trace of whip cream from his upper lip. "I think the sea food would have done you in eventually."

"You say eventually like that would have taken more than three days." She took another bite of waffle and smiled happily. Maybe they should eat here instead of at the guest house for the rest of their stay here. Seeing that he'd missed some of the cream, she reached out and used a thumb to get the rest of it. It was an entirely practical gesture that turned somehow more intimate than she intended. Something about the way his green eyes darkened and focused on her made her fidget, heat rising to her cheeks. Deliberately looking away, she licked the cream off her finger and continued in a studiously casual manner: "Besides, as trying as Aranhil can be at times, he's leagues better than Rane."

"I cannot disagree."

Very reluctantly, she checked the time via the pocket watch in her vest. Blast, it was already this late?

"We need to get back, don't we," Aran guessed without even craning his neck to look at the watch.

Grumbling, she shoved it back into her pocket. "Unfortunately."

"Cheer up. Twenty-eight days to go."

"That sounds absurdly longer than thinking of it as four weeks and I resent that." She polished off the last of her waffle, dragging it through dregs of whipped cream before popping it in her mouth. Then, nothing else for it, they battled their way back through the crowded market streets and to the guest house.

Neither of them spoke much on the way, but Aran linked arms with her again, which Sevana liked—quite a bit, truth be told. If she were lucky enough, perhaps Ursilla would focus on some part of her that wouldn't leave Sevana flat on her back for the next few days. She'd like to pursue this budding relationship.

They arrived at the guest house to find Ursilla already waiting. She regarded them with minimal patience, indicating she'd been waiting a while, and she announced with no fanfare or segue, "Let's tackle your magical core again."

Sevana couldn't contain a groan. Naturally, Ursilla decided it was time to tackle her magic core again. Her luck usually ran that good.

With her snack turning into a hardened lump in her stomach, Sevana stared at the woman with a flat, unhappy tilt to her mouth. To be hit with this news first thing was bad enough, but she'd hoped to go out and test a theory on the tubes. Not to mention other, equally pleasant activities that involved Aran. Being flat on her back while two different types of magic duked it out in her system sounded distinctly a less pleasant option.

Aran seemed to share her opinion, judging from the dark frown he sported, but he also looked resigned. They shared a look, and it was enough for Sevana to understand that he didn't like it either, but was there any point in putting it off further? It had to happen sometime.

"Alright." Sevana huffed out a breath and looked down at her shirt. This one wouldn't be easy to pull the collar down so that Aran had the right access. The material wasn't stretchy enough to accommodate that. "Let me change into something more workable."

12

Perhaps on the outside, Arandur looked calm. At least, he tried his best to appear that way, although he had no idea how effective his acting was. The last time they'd tackled Sevana's magical core, her body had not responded well, to put it mildly. The trouble she'd had with her senses lingered as well, not fully adjusted yet. He had known, or at least he'd thought he understood, just what this would entail going in. But the reality of it, being the instrument to slowly change Sevana over and seeing her suffer through the rebirth process, he hadn't been prepared for it. For that matter, Arandur didn't think he could even begin to prepare for it, even if he'd had a decade's worth of forewarning.

It was so much worse now. Bad enough when she was still a friend and a potential-something. But now? His heart twisted in an uncomfortable, sharp way in his chest when she came out of the bedroom, wearing her loosest and most malleable shirt.

His fingers latched onto the cold hilt of his dagger in stranglehold grip, but he couldn't force himself to draw it. A sick sense of premonition sat in his stomach like lead. Arandur intensely did not want to do this.

Something of that showed on his face, as Sevana went straight to him and poked him sharply in the ribs. "Don't stall. Nothing good will come of it."

Seriously, this woman. She met everything head-on. More than sweet words of reassurance, Arandur found this sharp prodding strangely more comforting. Or at least, he knew how to react better to it and his mouth twisted up in a brief smile that felt more like a grimace. "Are you really sure about this? Considering what happened last time—"

"Aran." Crossing her arms over her chest, she lifted both eyebrows in challenge. "Give me one advantage to putting this off."

Of course, he couldn't. Groaning, he gave in with a nod. "Fine. Ursilla, the same spot over her heart as before?"

"Yes."

Perhaps the women were sure of this. Arandur harbored his doubts, although he kept the rest to himself, and forced himself through the motions: draw the dagger, prick his index finger to draw just enough blood to the surface. The skin just above her heart was smooth and warm, as usual, and he focused very carefully on drawing out the design, as this was not something with a margin for error. If there was ever a time to execute something flawlessly, it was now.

He only breathed easy when the last lines of the design connected. Carefully withdrawing his hand, he absently focused a touch of healing magic on his finger to close up the open wound, his eyes never leaving her. To Arandur, he saw not only a world of skin, but the magical energy that made up Sevana herself. She was in a hybrid state, a flux of energies both Fae and human, the two magicks pressing up against each other in a clear bid for dominance. Just looking at her made him cringe instinctively on some level. Really, all things considered, it was amazing that she'd made it back up on her feet at all.

The blood on her skin slowly seeped in through the pores, and the reaction was sharp and obvious as his blood introduced more Fae energy into her system. The human magic reacted as if challenged to an open battle, struggling immediately against it. Arandur, having seen this reaction before, braced himself immediately for action.

Ursilla moved in closer, watching her and mouthing something to herself. It was not, unfortunately, in a language that Arandur spoke. Something far older, likely. Arandur wasn't sure if he was grateful that he couldn't understand her or not.

"This isn't good," Ursilla said slowly. She put a flat palm against

Sevana's skin, exactly where Arandur had drawn just a moment before, frowning in concentration. "Your magical core is reacting stronger than it did before. Why is it gaining strength instead of waning?"

"Human thing," Sevana answered, voice strained. Beads of sweat dotted her temples and forehead, the hollow of her throat, and her eyes dilated like a cat's in the dark. "We excel at the last-ditch effort. Ursilla, tell me this is one of those things that will get worse before it gets better."

Ursilla did not answer, which was alarming enough. She studied it for a while longer, then actively pushed her own magic into Sevana. Arandur shifted a half-step to the right, trying to see exactly what she was doing. If someone didn't explain it to Sevana soon, his very impatient Artifactor would lose what remained of her patience.

Glancing up, he saw that Sevana was staring hard at her own chest, as if trying to determine for herself what Ursilla was up to. Considering her eyes were still not right, he doubted that she could see much. "She's attempting to give the Fae blood within you an additional boost of power."

Sevana didn't even glance up. "Yes, I caught that much. Is it working?"

"I can't tell," Arandur admitted, as frustrated by this as she was. Put him in the woods, Arandur could track any living thing, could read the soil and water and the very wind to find his quarry without trouble. But he was not a magician, nor a loremaster, and this was far outside of his understanding. He could only report what his eyes saw, and in comparison to a loremaster, that wasn't much. "Your magical core is growing increasingly unstable, the power fluctuating in high arcs."

"Don't need to tell me that," Sevana gasped. Her back arced, a muted scream caught in the back of her throat.

Alarmed, Arandur instantly braced her with his own body, ready to keep her upright so that Ursilla could work. Although, really, couldn't they move this over to the bed? The couch? She'd do better horizontal. "Ursilla, perhaps she should be lying down?"

Withdrawing her hand, Ursilla nodded absently in agreement,

eyes still trained on Sevana's core. "Yes. I think this will be more of a battle than I'd bargained for. I did not expect this sort of resistance. Here, place her on the couch. Sevana, move slowly, I know that every nerve you have is alive right now with pain."

"Pain and really weird signals," Sevana agreed, panting out the words before biting at her bottom lip. She paused mid-step, eyes screwed tight for a long moment, then blew out explosively. "Black magic! Ursilla, for the record, accelerated transformation? I do not recommend it. Bad idea."

"I believe there is a reason why you're only the third to attempt it in known history," Ursilla agreed in a falsely mild tone.

Arandur appreciated their attempt at banter, as his nerves were stretched tight. He helped Sevana ease her way down onto the couch, mentally going through a list of what had happened last time. Loose clothes, cold cloths, gentle foods that she could easily digest—he could gather all of that up. Hopefully it would help, although even as he thought all of this, he watched Ursilla put her hand against Sevana's skin once more. Perhaps this time his Sevana wouldn't be laid out in a fetal position for the rest of the day.

She barely put her hand against Sevana's skin when both women froze, their eyes jerking up to look at each other.

"Get out," Sevana urged her strongly.

Wait, what?

Ursilla latched onto his wrist with strength a dragon would envy and hauled him bodily out the front door before he could even formulate a protest. "Ursilla! What's happen—"

The syllables still hung in the air when a concussive force of magic struck him sharply from behind. It burned him briefly, like steam from a magma vent, striking him off-balance. Staggering forward, Arandur barely kept his feet, his ears ringing. Shaking it clear, he turned and found the guest house now missing most of the roof, the door, and the front wall.

"I had a feeling," Ursilla muttered darkly, mostly in a rhetorical fashion.

Sevana sat on the floor, the couch obliterated into dust motes and kindling underneath her. A storm of magic and air whipped around her in a stream of contrasting colors and force, Fae and human magic bursting free of the core that should house it in a visible spectrum as they battled for dominance. Sevana's head was thrown back, mouth open in a silent scream, hands clutching at her chest.

Horrified, Arandur whipped about and demanded of Ursilla, "What can we do?!"

Ursilla stared hard at Sevana for an agonizingly long second, the wheels visibly spinning in her mind. "Her magical core is trying to reject the Fae blood."

Almost, almost, Arandur snapped at her: *Yes, that's bloody obvious, I can see what the problem is! Give me the solution!* He bit his lip hard enough to draw blood, keeping those words behind his teeth. Part of him recognized what Ursilla was doing—working through the problem out loud. Sevana sometimes did that. As irritating as that was, he couldn't yell at her now and expect her to think coherently with his voice blasting through her ears.

Although he still wanted to take her by the shoulders and shake her.

They both glanced up as the roof of the guest house abruptly splintered with a horrendous cracking sound, lifting up in the air, pieces of it caught and swirling in the magical maelstrom. The force of it was as strong as any windstorm that Arandur had ever witnessed and thinking of all of that pressure battling inside Sevana…it tore at his heart. Even if she survived the fallout of this magical duel of forces, the structure of the house was quickly tearing itself apart. What if some piece of it collapsed on top of her?

"I don't think we can just let her battle her way through this." Ursilla spoke quickly, half under her breath as if more to herself than to him. The way she stood, several feet from the ruined house, spoke of caution, but her eyes were glued to the kneeled form of Sevana on the floor. With no heed to the crowd of uneasy people gathering all around them, Ursilla gnawed on her thumbnail. "Her body won't be able to handle the pain and shock of this much longer; her heart might fail."

A few overheard her and gasped, then spoke in quick whispers to each other.

Arandur stoutly ignored them—ignored, too, his heart beating out a terrified tempo. "Ursilla, tell me what to do."

Those dark, sharp eyes of hers turned to him in a brutally honest evaluation. "You're sure that you can reach her? Even through that magical storm of power?"

Antsy, desperate to get in there, Arandur shifted from foot to foot and kept his answer as succinct as possible. "Yes."

"You might be correct." Ursilla returned to studying Sevana carefully. "You might be the only one, in fact. Both halves of her magic will recognize you. I'm afraid I have no neat solution to this, so listen carefully. You must inject her with your blood again. But this time, do so repeatedly until her magical core concedes the battle. You must override it. Do not stop, even if she screams or fights you. Time is not on our side in this."

Ursilla barely had the last word out before he moved, sprinting back inside, slipping the dagger free and slicing the tip of his finger open as he ran back in. The magical storm did not spare him, even if it did recognize him on some level. The wind battered him fiercely, bringing stinging tears to his eyes, ripping at his clothes and forcing his footsteps to slow. Arandur slogged his way forward, calves and thighs straining to push his way inside. More than once, something came whistling at him, a piece of wall or furniture, and he either had to duck or lift an arm to quickly block it. It left his forearms littered with bruises and shallow cuts.

Ignoring the minor pains, he bent forward, eyes opened in slits to help protect them from the fierce wind, forcing his way through the howling wind. His ears nearly bled in protest, the sound so horrendous, ears popping at the change in pressure. Eons passed in minutes as he finally made it to the eye of the storm. His heart broke to see Sevana hunched in, nearly fetal with pain. She didn't like to show weakness and yet tears poured down her cheeks and she openly sobbed when she could catch enough breath to do so. Bloody gashes decorated her chest where her nails had bit into the flesh. Animal instinct, trying to claw out the thing tearing her apart.

Arandur put his free hand over both of hers, drawing them down so that he could reach her chest. He half-expected a fight, because she was barely sensible, but her eyes tracked his movements. When he pulled her hands away, she allowed it, clutching at him in a grip sure to leave more bruises. The trust in that gesture nearly broke him as nothing else had.

Focusing solely on her bloodied skin, he quickly traced out the emblem. Her magic flared again in protest, hard enough that it wrenched Sevana's spine up in a snap, a scream rattling through her constricted throat. Arandur saw no progress because of his actions but Ursilla had been clear: Do not stop.

Grimly, he bent to the task and did it again. Then again. Wind and stars, he didn't think a human's power could be strong enough to battle Fae magic like this. Ursilla was right: why would an Artifactor's power be enough to fight his blood? A sorcerer's he could understand, but this? Sevana wasn't even particularly powerful for an Artifactor. Why?

Then again, no one had ever attempted to transform a human magician.

"Come on," he growled, mostly to the blood swirling about her magical core. The force of the wind was such that the words were snatched from his mouth and even he could barely hear himself. Arandur had to blink back more tears, eyes streaming in protest, and clear his vision so he could see what he was doing. "Come on, work!"

As if waiting for the command, his blood finally moved as it needed to, surrounding her magical core on all sides. It coated it thickly, like a plaster mold around unfired clay, not leaving any trace of her core visible on the outside. Arandur wanted to pause, to hold his breath and see if it would be enough, but he didn't dare. Ursilla's words still reverberating between his ears, he once again drew the symbol upon her chest. This time, even as he did so, the mad swirl of magic buffering him like a whirlwind slowly lost its fervor. The speed and intensity of it faded as it lost its force. Arandur dared a glance around them, measuring it with his eyes, and found that the destructive velocity and power was now halved, at least. A strong summer breeze had more force than this.

Sevana drew in a shaky breath, the first she'd managed in the past several minutes, then another, her lungs working frantically for air. Arandur scooted around on his knees, offering her his chest to lean against, and she took it, but stayed upright. The way she moved spoke of tender joints and muscles still aching with raw pain.

They both watched her magical core with baited breaths. The wild magic flaring out of her gradually drew back within her skin, as it should, then turned into a more muted glow as the Fae blood finally battled her magical core under submission. Arandur watched it sharply for several moments, but it seemed that they were finally over the worst of it. "Ursilla?" he called over his shoulder.

The elderly Unda scurried inside, carefully picking her way over the debris of the wall. What was left of it. Barely anything of the house still stood, aside from the kitchen area, which still had at least the base cabinets standing. Sitting on her haunches, she examined Sevana with hands and eyes, lips pursed as she did so. "Well. That didn't go at all as planned."

Sevana almost laughed, but it turned into a painful moan. "Don't make me laugh. That's not nice."

"I wasn't trying to, child," Ursilla returned tartly, but she smiled. "If you can laugh about this, you'll be fine. Don't scowl at me so, Arandur. She will be fine. I think, however, we'll delay the next few treatments until her body's recovered from this ordeal."

Arandur thought that went without saying, but was relieved to hear it regardless. "I think some healing is in order."

"Yes, quite. Let's—".

From the outside, a shrill voice demanded, "Sellion! What have you done to my guest house?"

Arandur glanced behind him to find Rane standing there with an incredulous look on her face, marred by the concern furrowing her brows together. Someone had reported to her the events of the last few minutes, but she obviously realized that Sevana hadn't chosen to break the building on purpose. Curano stood at his queen's elbow, also looking around in vague horror, although he seemed somewhat impressed by the sheer force of the destruction.

"Her magical core went berserk on this last treatment," Ursilla answered, slowly gaining her feet again, each movement speaking of compromised agility due to her age. "But not to fear, Rane, Curano. We've handled it, and I do not think she will cause an accidental explosion again. The healers are what she needs now."

One look at Sevana, still leaning weakly into Arandur, was enough for Rane. The queen nodded decisively. "Yes, that's quite clear. Here, take my cloak. Wrap it around her. I'll escort you to the healers myself. I cannot rest easy until I know that our guest is comfortable again."

"I will stay and oversee the repairs here," Curano informed his queen, still eyeing the area with a judicious look. "Our people need reassurance that this was not a disaster."

"That's an excellent plan, my dear," Rane approved.

Most of the time Rane annoyed Arandur. He found her shallow, somewhat flippant, and vain. But in this moment he could kiss her. For once, she was being helpful in all the right ways, and her very presence would make it clear to the healers that Sevana was to receive every possible care. He accepted the warm cloak, made of some furry creature by the feel of it, and wrapped it around Sevana carefully. Her body felt chilled to him and she clutched the cloak a little tighter to her before burrowing back into his arms.

"If I lift you, will you be alright?" he asked her softly.

"I think so," she whispered hoarsely. Her throat sounded as if it were raw, as it likely was. "No vertigo, at least."

"Alright, let's try it." Easing his arms under her knees and around her back, he brought her in close to his chest before lifting her up slowly. When she didn't flinch, he dared to think that she would be alright with a short trip to the healers.

Rane marched ahead of them like a standard bearer, shooing her people to either side to give them room. Ursilla hovered at his elbow, keeping a sharp eye on Sevana, which Arandur appreciated. She lay so still in his arms that he feared she'd fainted. Well, that might be a blessing in this circumstance, as she would need rest to recuperate.

Her breath gusted across the bare skin of his neck in a gentle rhythm. It reassured him more than any amount of words.

More than a few people had gathered to see what was going on, lining the street on either side, allowing the four to pass while gathering a look. They did not like the state of their Artifactor benefactor, the mothers especially, as they were fond of Sellion for bringing them their children. Those that were not on the streets hovered from above the air bubble, swimming along on top and following. It made for a strange procession.

A few matched Arandur's pace for a moment, offering any comfort or help they could, and Arandur patiently thanked them each time for the offer and promised to tell them when Sevana was awake again. It touched him that his sometimes prickly woman still made such deep ties of friendship in a foreign land, that relative strangers would feel the need to take care of her.

"She is well loved," Ursilla noted. Something in her voice sounded vaguely surprised. "I knew that she'd brought us some children, but…."

"She's done more for the Unda than that," Rane corrected, tilting her head to speak over her shoulder. "She's helped to guard our borders. She's taken an enemy out of our territory safely and made sure she was punished for her offenses. She's helped protect our land and people from a volcano up north, near Nanashi, and stayed to make sure that our land would recover afterwards. Sellion of South Woods is more than an ally, she is our friend. All of my people understand this."

"Which was why you called for me and demanded she be treated here," Ursilla completed wryly. "Yes, I now understand fully. You could have said all of this before, you know."

Rane shrugged, as if it wasn't really important. "You knew enough."

As if realizing, Ursilla looked sharply up at Arandur. "She has done the same for South Woods, hasn't she. That's why Aranhil was so keen to take her in as a new daughter."

"Something like it, yes. But in truth, even if she had not done so much for us, we would have loved her anyway."

Ursilla snorted, not entirely disbelieving, but clearly realizing that she had asked a man with a biased opinion. Well, not that Arandur could refute that. He was admittedly prejudiced where Sevana was concerned.

Someone must have raced ahead to alert the healers, as three stood in the doorway, obviously waiting on them. Arandur had not met these three women before but was reassured by their magical auras, so clearly suited to their profession.

They had the good sense to not try and take Sevana from him, instead directing him with gentle touches and softly voiced instructions to come this way. In his current state, Arandur's protective instincts ran hot, and just the idea of putting her down again did not sit well with him. He had to take many deep breaths to remind himself that it would be necessary to let others tend to her. It became a mantra in his head, although it took more than a few dozen repetitions to get it through to his instincts.

The air inside the domed-shaped building was perfectly clear, the walls and bedding a pure white, giving an ambiance of cleanliness and serenity. The building felt very large, enough to comfortably house dozens of patients, but they didn't take him far inside. They directed him to the first room on the right, and he went through, only noting the furniture enough to avoid smacking his shins into it. Single bed, two chairs, small chest of drawers next to the bed, a narrow table that spanned the foot of the bed.

Gently, he laid Sevana down. The youngest of the three healers helped to draw Rane's cloak off of her before returning it to the queen hovering in the doorway. Arandur stepped far back, to the corner of the room, allowing the three women to work. They clucked over the bloody claw marks in her skin, talking to themselves in a quick flurry of information and orders, hands moving and dispensing healing magic as they worked.

"Please, ladies," Rane chided them. "I understand one word in three. How is she?"

The eldest matron, who was likely pushing the boundaries of

elder, stepped away to answer. "She is alright, Rane. Her magical core is still transforming from its human origin, so we'll need to monitor her closely overnight. I think it will be complete by morning. Her heart suffered considerable strain from the stress. She's suffering from several wrenched and cramped muscles along her neck, spine, and thighs. But all of this can be dealt with. She'll need rest, quiet, and carefully dosed healing spells over the next two days."

Ursilla spoke for the first time, attention on Sevana. "I estimate we'll need to wait on her treatments for another three days."

"Likely five," the healer counselled. Like most selkies, she had dark hair, although hers was greyer at her age, pulled up in a sensible bun, complimenting the all-white dress she wore. The woman radiated competence and authority as she faced Ursilla down. "A human's heart is frailer than you'd think. I do not wish to make it arrest."

"Hmm, yes." Ursilla pointed a finger at Arandur, still lurking in the corner. "You'd best make arrangements. That one will not leave her side until she's able to walk out of here on her own."

The healer turned, slate-grey eyes sweeping him from head to toe, and the expression on her heart-shaped face turned matronly for a moment. "I know a losing battle when I see one. Are you banded, dear?"

Shaking his head, Arandur corrected her, "Courting."

"Ah. Still, a happy thing. It is your blood within her, is it not? I thought so. It's best you stay on hand then, anyway. If she does take a turn, we'll need your blood to help treat her. Unfortunately, pausing mid-transformation like this brings its own complications. Not that we can afford to keep pressing forward, not with her health in this state." Frowning, she gave Ursilla a reproachful look, full lips pulled tight. "You couldn't have paced this out a little more? She's a magician. With such complications—"

"I believe it would have been more dangerous to proceed any slower. And Sevana herself insisted on this timeline." Ursilla folded her arms over her chest and stared the healer down.

Shaking her head, the healer refused to be cowed and retorted, "As if patients know what's best for them. Not that there's much to argue at this stage, what's done is done. I hope, at least, that someone is taking notes on her progress?"

"I am," Arandur volunteered, half-lifting a hand. "I have it on me. Would you like to see it?"

"Well." Smiling at him, she crossed the three feet separating them. "You're well prepared. Yes, if you don't mind. It will give us an idea of what complications to expect tonight."

Arandur really did like the impression he received from this woman. She practically radiated competence. "Perhaps you'd help me go through them? I want to make this a record for future generations, if something like this happens again."

"Oh! Is that why you took the notes? Yes, quite clever. We'll want our own copy for the official records." Patting his arm, she took the slim journal and flipped to the first page. "I see. Hmm, yes, you've written what you could see, but a finer eye might be needed for this to make sense to a healer down the line. I'll help you from now on. I'm Elbereth."

"Arandur," he responded, feeling the tension slowly seep out of him. "A pleasure to meet you."

"And you. Let's make sure your Sevana is comfortable, hmm? And then we'll see to you. You're a little drained after all of that and I want a better look at the wounds on your arms."

Wearily, he nodded. With Sevana in such capable hands, he could afford to sit down and let someone else take charge for a few minutes.

13

Sevana awoke to snoring.

As annoying as she normally found that, this time it made her smile because she knew instantly who it was: Aran. He claimed (quite adamantly) that he didn't snore. And normally he didn't, she could agree on that point, but when he became truly stressed and tired he sounded like a hibernating bear with a sore tooth. Like now.

Gingerly opening her eyes, she turned her head in slow degrees, feeling as if her entire body had been tenderized. The last steak she had eaten suddenly gained her sympathies. Fortunately, the room was not brightly lit, sparing her poor eyes, and Aran was not far. Someone had brought a second cot in and snugged it in between her bed and the wall. He was stretched across it, fully clothed, a blanket haphazardly draped over his legs. His dark hair stuck up in every possible direction, and for a moment he looked bed-rumpled and cute with it.

That's how Sevana knew her brains had been scrambled. She did not think in terms of cuteness.

A soft tread of shoes stole into the room, and a light, feminine voice inquired, "Are you awake, Artifactor?"

Turning her head the other direction was quite a chore, but Sevana forced her way through the motion, feeling her hair snag a little underneath her shoulders as she moved. The woman leaning over her was nearly retirement age, her experience written in fine lines around her eyes and mouth and in the iron grey hairs weaving through her dark hair. Sevana blinked, startled that she could now clearly see every trace of magic within this woman, every elemental core that made up an Unda's being. It had been a hazy blur of mixed elemental magic to her before. Was this what a Fae could see?

"Artifactor?" she prodded again, gently and with an understanding smile.

Wool-gathering. Wonderful. She really had been knocked arse over tea kettle, hadn't she? "Yes. I'm awake. Just not fully aware."

"Well, you answered in complete sentences, so you're doing better than expected," she said reassuringly. "I'm Elbereth, Head Matron here. You've been asleep twelve hours, without our intervention, which is quite wonderful. You're likely feeling very fatigued and sore. We did have to reset some of your sockets, as your ankles were just out of joint, as was your spine. Your tendons also were stretched to the snapping point. We've mitigated the worst of the damage to your musculature but you'll need a few more days of bedrest to heal from the events of today. Your core, I am happy to say, is now stabilized and portrays nothing more than Fae magic."

Sevana tried to peek down at herself but the angle was too awkward and she quickly gave that up. Later, when she could sit up properly, she'd try again. "Truly, my magical core isn't fluctuating? At all?"

"Not a trace of human magic left within you. We're actually quite pleased at the outcome, at least in that sense. Perhaps because of your ordeal, however, your core isn't quite as strong as anticipated. You're at a pre-teen level." Perhaps reading the dismay all over her face, Elbereth quickly tacked on, "But I also believe that it's not able to gain full strength in your current body. If you were to harbor a fully developed magical core, it would wreak havoc on the parts of your body that are still human. As you transform fully into Fae, I believe that the rest of you will grow to suit."

That did sound completely reasonable. Sevana chose to believe it and nodded in a shallow dip of the head. "I believe you're right. How is Aran?"

"He's fine," Elbereth answered with a fond smile over at the sleeping man. "He stayed up initially, and walked me through the record, but I convinced him to lay down about six hours ago. He's very drained from what he did earlier. I expect both of you will need a few days to properly recover from it."

Sevana had not been blind to what Aran was going through while trying to subdue her wildly out of control magic. She hadn't been able to speak or reason, not when wracked with that kind of pain, but she hadn't been oblivious either. Seeing him next to her, nearly comatose with fatigue, did not surprise her. Hearing that he would recover with rest was reassuring, though. Sometimes that sort of magical and blood drain required intervention from a skilled healer to offset problems.

Something Elbereth had casually dropped looped back around in Sevana's brain. "What record?"

"You didn't know? Arandur is keeping a detailed record of everything you experience as you're transformed."

Sevana had certainly seen him scribbling away in a journal and assumed he was doing something, but hadn't asked. The man was allowed some privacy, even if she'd been very curious. Sevana, of course, had been keeping her own records, but truly, Aran's would be interesting in their own right. He could see far more of her transition than Sevana herself could. And with his outside perspective, he might be the more impartial observer as well. "I'd like to see it."

"I'm sure. I'm having it copied now so that we can keep a record of it. I'll bring it back when it's done." Elbereth lifted Sevana's wrist and checked pulse and temperature, then helped lift her head enough that she could drink most of a carafe of water.

Sevana had no idea how thirsty she was until that cool, blissful liquid slid down her throat. She settled back into the pillow with a sigh. But the water made her realize that she'd missed dinner the night before, and it was time for breakfast now, and her stomach gave a petulant grumble. "Can I eat?"

"Something soft and easily digestible," Elbereth answered with a judicious look at her. "You're not feeling nauseous? Then I'll have the kitchens bring something to you. If you feel like you can eat, you should. It will help speed along your recovery. I'll send word to both Ursilla and Rane that you are awake. They might want to see you today."

Having several questions without answers, and being stuck in bed for the foreseeable future, Sevana privately admitted that she would prefer to have them come to her. "That's fine."

"Rest until then." With an approving nod—Elbereth apparently was pleased at her status—the head matron swept back out of the room.

Sevana let out a low breath of air, relaxing into the pillows fully. Every caution about changing a magician into a Fae now made perfect sense. Even with a skilled and experienced Unda mother overseeing her every step of the way, her magical core had still exploded. It scared her, even now, to think of what might have happened.

And she really, truly, had to beat sense into Aran's head. An intelligent person did *not* just walk up to someone while their magic went into some sort of catatonic breakdown and…and…

The thought sputtered to a cold stop. She knew very well why he'd done it. And she knew very well that without that interference, she'd be dead by now. Even if the magical overload hadn't killed her, Sevana's heart wouldn't have been able to put up with the strain for much longer. Her heart would have shattered under the extremity, killing her near instantly. Faced between the possibility of suffering severe damage himself, or watching her die a violent death in front of his eyes, Aran, of course, chose the former.

Despite what people thought of her, she wasn't blind. Sevana knew very well that Aran adored her. She was less confident as to *why*, but his devotion couldn't be missed or misunderstood. It spoke volumes that he always chose to stay with her, but the events of this morning made it abundantly clear that if asked, Aran would lay his life on the line for her without hesitation.

Never in Sevana's wildest dreams had she believed that romance would be part of her life, but stonking deities, she apparently had the opportunity now. The way he kept breaching her personal space said that Aran liked the skinship with Sevana, which was good, as she certainly enjoyed it. Again, she didn't understand why he'd kissed her that one time—for once in her life, Sevana regretted not properly paying attention to a conversation—but he hadn't stopped his affectionate touches. Excellent sign, that. It meant that her chances of talking him into courting were much better than she'd initially assumed. If she played her cards right, of course.

And then, if she were very clever indeed, they might make it safely through the courting stage without him wanting to strangle her by the end of it.

Oh, stars. She really did have it bad for him, didn't she? She was literally lying here plotting how to be on her best behavior while courting him. If Sarsen or Kip saw her now, they'd be laughing themselves hoarse.

Sevana abruptly decided that all of this business was Aran's fault. If he weren't so charming, and intelligent, and patient, and… well, and Arandurish, she wouldn't have been attracted to him. Or contemplating courting. Therefore, it was Aran's fault, and it would certainly be his fault if things went sideways.

Although she'd really rather they didn't go wrong.

Someone stepped lightly through the door and Sevana turned her eyes up to track her new visitor. Ursilla paused at her bedside, looking her over carefully. "You're awake. Good."

"I think," Sevana's voice came out raspy, still sore from all the screaming the night before, "that I now understand why the old tales cautioned against changing someone with human magic in them."

"Yes," Ursilla agreed, utterly deadpan, "the logic behind that is quite obvious now. I believe that without Arandur's dogged persistence, you would not be alive. I do not know of many who would charge into such a maelstrom of magic."

"The one thing I've never questioned is Aran's courage," Sevana answered with a faint smile. "His common sense, maybe, but never his courage."

"Nor his devotion," Ursilla tacked on, expression insinuating a great deal. "I now understand why Aranhil had such complete faith that he would stay with you throughout this process."

Funny, how none of them had questioned that. Sevana hadn't even wondered why Aran leapt to volunteer. But she decided that was enough sentimental thoughts on her end for the day and led the conversation in a different direction. "Now that my magical core is finally stable, do you expect any trouble with the rest of the transformation?"

Shaking her head, Ursilla denied, "No. At least, nothing that could compare to what happened this morning. We might have some strange hiccups, such as what you experienced with your senses, but that's a normal enough reaction, considering how rushed we're doing things. I believe that you are now over the worst of it."

Sevana let out a sigh of relief. "You've no idea how glad I am to hear that. Do I dare try to work magic?"

"Not at this time," Ursilla warned, her tone cautionary. "Your body is too unstable, and it would be hard on your magical core to attempt even basic spells. I know you've been practicing with Arandur, but let's put that on hold for now. Perhaps turn your attentions elsewhere. There's no harm in learning the magical theory at this point. In a week or so, once your body is more attuned with your core, we can revisit the idea of perhaps doing elementary magic."

More or less the answer she expected. Sevana nodded in acceptance. "Fine. Magical theory it is. How mad is Rane about me melting her guest house?"

"Not at all. She was beside herself with worry, and checked on you several times this morning. I sat with her as she composed a message to Aranhil reporting what had happened with reassurances that you were recovering. Curano was actually impressed with the level of destruction. Aside from the guest house, you damaged four other neighboring houses as well." Ursilla paused and added oh-so-casually, "A note from you would also be helpful in appeasing Aranhil, I think."

"In other words, please write him so he doesn't try to charge down here himself," Sevana translated dryly and without any effort. "Yes, yes, alright. Give me some paper and a pen, I'll jot him a note. I'd like to send one to my master as well. I haven't written him in the past week and he's likely getting antsy. Or better yet, fetch me a mirror. No, on second thought, it would be better if they don't see me like this. Let's stick with letters."

Pleased with how agreeable she was being, Ursilla sailed off to go fetch things.

Something about the exchange woke Aran up and he lurched half upright, propped on one elbow while struggling to keep his eyes open. They kept falling shut before he wrenched them wide again. "Sev?"

Taking the hand reaching for her, she squeezed it gently. "I'm alright. Magic core's stable. Go back to sleep."

At her reassurance, he grunted, a sleepy and pleased smile on his face as he collapsed back down on the bed. In two seconds, he went right back to snoring.

Shaking her head, Sevana chuckled in low amusement. Had he really even been awake? Somehow, she doubted it. In fact, she made a personal bet with herself right there that she would have to repeat that conversation with him once he properly woke up again.

Ursilla came back in with a portable writing desk, a curious look on her face. "Did I hear Arandur speaking?"

"He was awake for about two seconds," Sevana answered, extending both hands and taking the portable writing desk from her. "I assured him I was alright and he was back asleep in the next second. I swear to you, he won't retain a word I said and we'll have to repeat it when he wakes up again."

"No doubt," Ursilla agreed peaceably, not all concerned about it. "I'm surprised he awoke at all."

"You and me both." Sevana drew out paper and pen and settled herself to write a very brief note of assurance. She didn't have the strength or mental stamina required to write a full on letter, and it likely wasn't necessary anyway. Rane and Ursilla would have given a proper account. All Sevana needed to do was give assurances.

Master's letter was where she put the bulk of her words; he would need more information to go from, as hers was the only account he'd likely see. Sevana made a mental note to copy both her record and Aran's to send along to him the next time she wrote. Master would be very grateful to see the details of her transformation and, truthfully, Sevana wanted a record of this in human hands. It had been the downfall of more than one race that they only kept records in their own cities, with their own experts. When that civilization fell, there was no one to pass their knowledge onto, and future generations had to re-learn it all the hard way. This might be the only occasion where a human could learn some of the secrets of the Fae, and if ever there was something to teach humanity about the Fae, it was certainly this.

Sevana, of course, would not mention why she would make another copy of the record, or who she was sending it to, as no doubt many of the Unda and the Fae would have a very different opinion than hers on this subject. But it was her body, her transformation, and none of their business who she told about it.

She also had no intention of asking permission.

14

After three days Sevana had finally recovered enough to become restless in her sickbed. Fortunately, she'd had enough busy work, what with copying the records and studying her new Fae magic, to keep her occupied while lying flat on her back. Still, it brought home to her the simple things that she missed. Normally if she were flat on her back like this, Baby and Grydon would curl up around her feet to keep her company. She missed furry bodies and thumping tails. She missed Big whispering to her.

On the last day of strict bed rest, she found herself more restless than usual. Aran either realized this or expected it, as he sat right at her bedside and gently massaged her legs, arms, and hands, working some of the residual tension from the muscles. Sevana enjoyed the attention, no doubt, as his warm hands felt good on her cool skin and he certainly knew what to do with them. "I wish I could return the favor."

He gave her that small, pleased grin that flashed in his tanned skin. "You will when you have the strength to do it. Maybe when we're home again."

"Home," Sevana sighed with true longing. "I miss the most ridiculous things about home. Grass. Sunlight. The wind whispering through the trees. Not to mention my bed."

"Really?" Aran's eyes crinkled up, head canted in teasing question. "That's what you're thinking about? Haven't you realized the obvious?"

"What obvious…" she trailed off as another thought occurred to her. "I'll be Fae when I return. I want to punch myself, how *stupid*. I'll be Fae! I can properly talk to Baby, Big, and Grydon, just as you do. Blast, why didn't I think of that before?"

Amused, he gave a rumbling chuckle. "I kept waiting for you to realize it. Of course, in your defense, you've had a great deal to manage and think about down here."

Sevana was still irked with herself. She should have realized all of that much sooner. "Poor Big has had to strain himself for years to speak to me. He's basically shouting whenever he communicates. This will be such a blessing for both of us."

"Funny, how you think of Big and not Baby."

Snorting, she retorted dryly, "Please. It doesn't take a mind reader to know what that oversized cat is thinking. I raised him; I know very well what he's up to most of the time."

His thumbs moved gently along the palm of her hand, stretching and releasing the buildup of tension there. In the past few days, all she had been able to do was read or write, and as a consequence of that, her hands hadn't been able to recover like the rest of her body. "I look forward to showing you the world again through your new senses. It's so much richer than you think it is."

"I look forward to it," Sevana answered honestly. "That, and re-learning magic. With all of the magic theory you and Ursilla have taught me in the past three days, it's become clear to me that I'd jumped to a conclusion that I shouldn't have. Master and I both did."

Pausing, he glanced up at her through his unfairly long, dark lashes. "What's that?"

"We both assumed that if I became Fae, I closed the chapter in my life where I was an Artifactor. But it's really not at all true. Fae magic is elemental, yes, but you still have to understand power balance and compatibility, and everything else that an Artifactor takes into consideration when performing magic." She warmed to her subject as excitement buzzed through her. "Rather, it'll be easier for me now to see exactly what I'm working with. I won't need to rely on instruments and gauges to tell me how powerful something is, I can literally just look at it and see for myself."

Aran paused again, watching her carefully, his anticipation seasoned with caution. "But human magic is different from Fae magic."

With her free hand, she waved this off. "Yes, yes, I know. But don't you see? Human magic is used to direct or combine other forces of power. Human magic is, to put it crudely, glue. Or direction. We use the powers of the world around us to do our bidding, and our instruments are only instruments to capture and direct that force. I won't be able to make tools as I did before, true enough, but with Fae magic at my disposal, I can make things that are *better*. Superior in every sense of the word. And really, half the time my work isn't making tools anyway. The past four years or so, I've been called upon to solve magical problems more often than not."

"And with your new magic, that will be even easier," Aran finished for her, his smile reflecting her delight. "I see. That's what you're truly excited about. You have absolutely no intention of ever living solely in South Woods, do you?"

"That sounds boring," Sevana informed him cheerfully. "Let's not."

Shaking his head, he barked out a laugh. "Poor Aranhil. He'll never get his wish, will he?"

"Not getting everything he wants is good for him."

Rolling his eyes, Arandur placated her. "Yes, yes."

⬤

That night they led her to a new guest house with what few belongings had survived the magical maelstrom and let her recover some more in a private setting, which she appreciated. Not only because people stopped dropping by so frequently with gift baskets, but also because the skinship with Arandur resumed. He'd not been as physically affectionate with her during her medical stay, understandably enough, but Sevana had half-feared that he wouldn't resume again. And that would be detrimental to her plans, as she didn't know how to pick up that thread once it was dropped.

But on the first night in the new guesthouse, he gave her a very sweet kiss goodnight on the cheek, which pleased Sevana enormously. Excellent. Plan Seduce Aran could commence without issue.

By the fifth morning, she got up and felt immeasurably better. Her head no longer had that light feeling, as if she were on the verge of fainting. Only a vague feeling of soreness lingered in her muscles, and she had energy to actually get dressed and possibly work. Sevana stared down at her own magical core, evaluating it thoughtfully as she put the last comb in her hair. It looked far better than it had five days ago. In fact, the swirl of elemental magic was bright and strong, stable in a way that it hadn't been for the past six months.

A light tap on the door announced Aran's presence and he leaned against the jamb, watching her. "How are you this morning?"

"Well enough that I want to work." She eyed him in return, not sure if she would have to argue that point or not. When he only cocked his head, expression reflecting hope back at her, the tension in her shoulders dropped. No argument, then? "You won't try to stop me, I take it."

"You're far more stable, magically speaking, than you have been in several months," he observed logically. "At least now you can work magic without accidental explosions. You've been learning magical theory for the past few days, too, so I'm sure you're itching to try out at least basic spells and get a firmer grip on how to do things. Just take it easy today, that's all I ask. I don't want you springing ahead like you're fully recovered and then relapsing."

Sevana snorted. "I'm not that foolish. But I want to go speak with Loman. He might have had a breakthrough while I was stuck in a bed, and if nothing else, he was supposed to talk to the head engineer over at the Kesly Station and see if their problem overlapped with ours, and if the solution we figured out here worked for them. If I need to go over there and fix their station too, I want to know it now and be able to plan ahead."

Shrugging agreement, Aran lifted himself away from the wall. "Breakfast first, then let's go."

Amenable to this, she followed him to the small kitchen table in the back of the guest house—nothing more than a wide board with two stools, really—and dished up the clam soup and flaky flatbread. Khan had left it for them this morning, along with fresh towels. Sevana was glad to still have their young host. The thought of breaking in someone new irritated her. The food was well-made, their cook a good one, but still… "If I never have seafood again after this, for as long as I live, it'll be too soon."

"Tell me about it," Arandur groaned in agreement, and Sevana noted that he did not have any of the soup, just the flatbread and tea for breakfast. "I'm very glad that you didn't get suckered in by Rane and choose to turn Unda instead."

"You're glad? I'm glad! I can't imagine staying under the waves the rest of my life and having such a limited diet." Shuddering in true horror, she forced herself to eat the first bite. It really wasn't bad, it was just that she had eaten so many clam and fish dishes over the past three weeks that she could barely get herself to eat any of it. But she had to, the transformation process was very demanding on her physically, and keeping her body well fueled was essential. "I vote we have lunch in the market."

"Seconded. For that matter, you still have more shopping to do."

"I won't have time for it this morning, though. Maybe later this afternoon."

Breakfast felt like torture, but she grimly powered through it, relieved when she could stack the empty dishes in the sink. They left for the station, which was a bit further of a walk, as the new guest house resided three streets away from the old one. Sevana noted the pedestrians they passed on the street, and their curious looks at her, but no doubt they'd all heard some garbled account of what had happened and were now satisfying their curiosity by getting a good look at the two who had melted a house.

Ignoring them, she focused on the first stage of her Seduce Aran Plan. So far, he had always initiated their contact, and certainly Sevana had been agreeable to it, but she felt like things were too one-sided to continue. If she was to show interest, then surely that meant initiating something. It felt awkward, as she'd never done anything of this nature before, but even she had held hands with people.

Young people, generally. But still.

Braving it, she tentatively slid her hand into the one hanging loose at Aran's side. His head snapped sharply around at the touch, but even through his surprise, Sevana read his delight. The broadest smile stretched across his face from ear to ear as his fingers closed around hers. Satisfied she'd succeeded, she smiled back and made sure to keep her hand in his right up until they reached the station.

It felt odd, holding hands with someone who had a larger hand than hers. She'd always been the larger person, holding a child's hand, and this role reversal brought a different emotional dynamic. Strangely, she felt as if she were being protected, instead of being the protector. An odd feeling, and Sevana didn't know what to do with it, although she eventually settled and decided she didn't mind it. Her hand felt very cold in comparison to his, and she strangely felt like apologizing for it, and might have if she'd been able to come up with words that didn't make her sound utterly foolish, even in her own head.

Aran didn't seem to mind any of this, though, as he moved just that half step closer so that their shoulders brushed together, letting their hands swing a little back and forth, playfully. It settled the butterflies in her stomach and she grinned back up at him, determined to just enjoy the moment.

Loman was loading into a pod as they approached, his back to her, and she broke the hold with Aran in order to skip ahead and stop him. "Wait, Loman!"

The head engineer twisted about in his seat to see who hailed him. More than a touch surprised, he greeted, "Artifactor! You're well enough to be up?"

"Yes, thankfully. Any more bedrest and I'd have gone perfectly mad. I'm glad I caught you. What are you doing?"

"Another test." He gestured her in. "Come, join me. We've levelled out most of the tunnels, at least the main three here at the station, and we're about to see if the pod will be sucked into another branch again, or if we've completely solved the issue."

Since she wanted to see that for herself, Sevana obligingly got in, Aran sitting close enough to her that their thighs pressed together. As he settled, the top of the pod came up and latched into place with a hiss of displaced air. Sevana, as much as she had worked on the problems here, had never actually ridden in one of the tubes. Her senses roved around, taking in things as she hadn't been able to before, as her human senses hadn't been quite up to the task. Now, with her Fae-enhanced eyes and ears, she could discern things in much more detail.

"Loman. I thought this pod was made of hardened glass," she said slowly, looking all around them at the transparent walls, "but it's not. It's fused quartz, isn't it?"

Bobbing his head in agreement, he gave her a curious look. "Your eyes are well now, I take it?"

"Yes, quite. My senses are in full working order—fortunately, as apparently I failed to ask an obvious question." Reaching up with her fingertips, she lightly grazed the quartz, so perfectly formed into a circle, and instinctively reached into the rock. Aran had explained to her that the Fae did not see the world as a human did. That they were more in tune with their surroundings, able to communicate with every element in some form or fashion. That was never clearer to her than in this moment, when the quartz reached back. It couldn't form words as a human could, it didn't have that kind of intelligence. It left impressions upon her instead—of extreme heat, a long period of coolness in a dark place, then more heat and a shaping will, creating what was around her today. It couldn't tell her much more than that, and she withdrew thoughtfully. "That was…something."

Aran beamed at her. "You're a natural."

Snorting, she tried to hide how pleased she was at that praise. "I've seen you do it often enough. But I now understand the problem better. Fused quartz has the same hardness as a steel file. Nothing in this tunnel or along the sea bed will have sufficient strength to leave a mark on it."

"Hard to tell how it's getting stuck because of that," Loman agreed sourly. "I assume there's something about the tunnel that's doing it. I just don't see any marks to offer us a clue."

"Frustrating," she agreed absently, mentally intrigued. Had the slope pushed the bottom of the tunnel upwards? Even an inch would do it. The confines of the tunnel were quite narrow, after all.

The end of the tube closed, leaving them in the dim lighting of the tunnel. Only the florescent rocks embedded in the walls provided any light whatsoever, a somewhat eerie glow of white and bright green that made everyone look sallow. Sevana's ears popped as the air pressure around them changed, and the pod lifted from where it rested on the ground. Not by a large margin, just enough to be felt. In the next second they abruptly moved forward, the pod rapidly picking up speed so that the light around them became streamlined, creating a somewhat beautiful and captivating display. Sevana had never seen the like before and enjoyed the novel transportation system for a moment.

"We've made some progress while you were recuperating," Loman informed her without any prompting. "It's been quite blissful, actually, finally having a solution, even if it turned out to be partial."

Sevana's attention snapped back to him. "Partial? Ah, you mean the pods that are still getting stuck midway?"

"Yes, them," Loman agreed with a grimace. "But correcting the slope seems to have solved the problem of them shooting off down the wrong branches, at least. We've run multiple tests on the first tube, and I'm doing the third run down this one. Pol has already done multiple trips on the third, or tried, but he keeps getting stuck at a certain point and it's been quite the task hauling him back again. For that matter, this tube gets stuck every time at a certain spot. Fortunately, it's not far past the reef, and it's easy enough for me to haul it back myself."

"But the intersecting tube that liked to abscond with the pods is before the reef?" Arandur inquired.

"Yes, which is why we decided to test it. If this run goes smoothly, we'll know the problem is fixed. At least, *that* problem is fixed." Loman's smile was rueful, a mixture of satisfaction and frustration, which was perfectly understandable.

"How about the other stations?" Sevana leaned forward on the narrow bench seat, very interested in any news. "Did you report our findings here?"

"I did, that very day," Loman assured her. "And they promptly went out to measure the land and discovered the same issues there. I'm not surprised by that, as I see that you're not, but I'm happy to report that the solution here seems to be working elsewhere. At least on this particular problem, we can assure our passengers that if they wish to get to Kesly Station, they'll actually reach Kesly instead of some other random destination."

"If they don't get stuck on the way," Aran pitched in wryly.

Loman's face screwed up in a pinched manner. "Yes, quite. I do wish we could figure out what's stopping us there. We've measured the land even more carefully after discovering the slope had changed, sure that if we levelled things perfectly, it would solve the problem. Unfortunately, we've had no such luck. I'm quite at my wit's end, Artifactor. I don't know what else to try."

"Well, I've spent several days away from the problem, I'll have a fresh perspective on it." Sevana didn't discount the importance of being an impartial observer. Sometimes it was possible to get too close to the problem to see the obvious.

Loman's head came up, eyes darting to the side. "That was the intersecting tunnel. We passed it without issue."

"Good." Sevana meant it, as that meant she only had one problem left to focus on. "And when do you normally get stuck?"

"Right about…now."

The pod abruptly slowed, then came to a swift halt. Sevana looked all around her, not able to discern what had changed. The clear transparency of the quartz allowed her to see the basalt nature of the tunnel around them, but even with her enhanced eyes, there was no obvious impediment. "It felt like we rammed into an obstacle of some sort."

"It did, didn't it," Loman agreed darkly. His frustration was clearly evident in the contortion of his features. "But if you come back to this spot and check, absolutely nothing bars our way. I can guarantee this. You see now why we believe so strongly that there must be something about the slope of the land that's causing this. Perhaps the tubes have been tilted and warped? But every measurement we've tried says they are exactly where they've always been, running in the same straight lines as they've done before. I really am out of ideas on why this is happening."

Sevana pursed her lips thoughtfully. But an outside examination wouldn't tell them if the floor of the tunnel had changed because of the sloped ground. Or was it some other problem, also not discernable from the outside? "Is it possible to get out at this point?"

"Unfortunately not, the air is still vacuumed around us. It would not be wise to exit the pod. In fact, you would have to break the pod to manage it."

"Then we'll have to come back by foot. I want to examine the tunnel more carefully. There has to be a reason here, we're just not asking the right question." Sevana stared at the walls around them, grinning and rubbing her hands together in evil glee. She so loved a problem that didn't have an obvious solution. "Well, alright, let's get back to the station."

Loman nodded, relaxing back in his seat, for all the world like a man waiting.

Dark suspicions formed. "Loman. When you said it was 'easy enough to get back' to the station, you didn't mean that you had to wait for a rescue party, did you?"

"Well, of course. It's not like I can manage anything while stuck in here. You can't call for help, or send up a signal flare. When we fail to reach the next station in the next twenty minutes, they'll realize that we got stuck again and send out a rescue party for us." He cocked his head at her. "Isn't that obvious?"

Sevana sank in on herself with a groan. "You're Unda! You seriously can't manage to get out of here on your own?"

"Not without tearing everything apart and drowning you two in the process," he answered, sounding amused. "If you think you can hold your breath for about twenty minutes and swim back, I'll give it a try."

Sevana glared at him darkly. More fool her for not asking questions and just blithely climbing in. Next time, she'd demand details first.

It took two hours of concentrated effort to haul the pod inch by inch back to its dock at the station. Sevana fumed the entire time, irritated that she was not only stuck in there without a viable means out, but stuck in there without anything to do. And the air got hot and stale very quickly, making it even more irritating. She yanked off her jacket to combat the heat, and Loman threw out a spell now and again to help refresh the air, but the entire experience remained bitterly unpleasant.

The next time they had to test the pods, Loman was going by *himself*.

Perhaps to soothe her irritation, Aran took her out of the guest house and down to the international market for an early dinner. She ordered three waffles with all of the cream and strawberries the plate could hold, devouring it without an ounce of guilt. Sugar assuaged her mood and she looked up, licking her bottom lip free of any trace of cream before asking, "Well. What shall we do with ourselves for the rest of the day?"

Holding his glass of tea with both hands, Aran eyed her with a very enigmatic expression in response. "I feel like this is a stupid question, but I'll ask it anyway. How would you like to spend a little time on a practical lesson in your new magic?"

"You know, Aran, I do believe you're right. I agree with that assessment." Standing abruptly, Sevana caught his hand and pulled him from the chair. "Come on, quick smart."

Chuckling, he allowed himself to be tugged, but he only let her tow him so far before he switched up and took lead, taking her away from the residential area of the city. Well, as far as the air bubble around them would allow. Only so much area was enclosed, after all. Still, he managed to find an area that had no buildings immediately nearby, in a small park-like area with two benches, a table, and a garden of sea anemones lining the beds. The area could just fit inside Sevana's workroom inside of Big, it was so small, but likely would work for their purposes.

Aran drew her down to sit on edge of the air bubble, close enough that she could put a hand right through the barrier if she chose to. He sank down on his haunches next to her, one hand resting on the small of her back. "Let's try something easy first. Water and air are the most versatile of all the elements, as they are, by nature, always in motion. They like to move, they adore direction, and are generally eager to obey. See if you can call a handful of water to you."

Despite all of the reading and lectures she'd received on how to do this, Sevana really only had working theory on how to accomplish even the most simple of tasks. She did remember that focused will came into it, as well as simple and easy instructions. Surely the most simple of those was 'come.' As long as she didn't accidentally bring a tidal wave down on their heads. Sevana was actually quite nervous about doing that. She had no good feel for how much was 'too much' power at this point. She was still growing accustomed to the new magical core in her chest.

Holding a hand directly ahead of her, she cupped it in preparation, then looked dead ahead at the patch of sea in front of her eyes. Right, focused intent. This was harder than it looked, as Sevana had always had tools and spoke incantations to guide her magic into the right paths before. Doing it all silently and without aids felt very, very strange to her.

"No," Aran corrected gently, shifting his weight to lean a touch closer. "Don't command, ask."

Right. Right, the elements had their own intelligence. She couldn't just point and snap her fingers like before. Blowing out a breath, she shoved any hint of frustration to the side and tried again. But this time, she tried to listen as well as communicate.

It was ever so faint, but the water ahead of her fingers rippled. A murmur, not of words, but of impressions—cold, together, movement. Yes, movement. Some of you, come here to rest.

Despite her focus, or perhaps because of it, she nearly leapt out of her own skin when a spray of water whipped out and splashed up against her clothes, neck, and face. Blinking, she spat it out and wiped at her eyes and mouth. "That was not at all what I wanted, thank you very much."

Snickering, Aran gave her a supportive pat on the back. "But at least it came. Just a little too eagerly. Try again?"

Determined, Sevana stretched her hand out again to the sea. She'd get this down, she would, and then she would call to wind next. And then earth. Sevana would keep listening and striving until she could speak to the world like the Fae she was becoming.

Tapping his hand between her shoulder blades, Aran murmured against her temple, "Don't stress. Relax. The elements are your friends now, remember. Breathe and let them come to you."

Sevana forced her shoulders to unclench from around her ears. "That is much easier in theory than in practice."

"Which is why we're practicing. Now, try again."

15

At three o'clock in the morning, Sevana's eyes snapped open. She lay rigid in the bed, her brain swirling as the obvious hit her: She knew exactly why the pods got stuck in the tunnel.

Then she groaned in the darkness, vexed beyond belief that her back-brain chose to pipe up *now*, in the dead of night, when she couldn't feasibly go out and test the theory.

Cloth shuffling around clued her in that Aran had heard her, and she looked up expectantly toward the doorway as he came through it. Anticipating his worry even before he got a word out, she held up a hand. "I'm fine. I just realized what the problem is with the tunnels. And why my brain decided to inform me of it *now* is an excellent question."

"Didn't you tell me once that your most brilliant ideas always come in the dead of night?" he asked. His voice was thick with sleep, but still lilted in amusement as he came to sit next to her on the bed, their hips pressed together.

"Yes," she growled, vexed about that. "And it's very frustrating. I used to keep notes next to my bed about my best ideas, but they were completely illegible the next morning."

"Sounds like you. Not that your handwriting is all that legible even when you are properly awake."

She smacked him in the arm for that, which he half-dodged, chuckling. "Why do I like you, again?"

"My devastating charm," he riposted, his grin barely visible in the dim lighting of the room. "Well? Don't leave me in suspense, what's the problem?"

Pursing her lips together, she stared at him and debated on whether or not she'd tell him tonight. He was being mischievous and Sevana was of half a mind to let him stew as punishment. In the end, she couldn't help herself, and told him anyway. "I believe the tunnels have compressed."

He cocked his head at her. "A rock is a very rigid body. I wouldn't think there was enough pressure to do that?"

Before he could trot the objection out, she was already shaking her head. "No, think about this. The weight of the water above us is crushing. Literally. It's very, very heavy and even a rock wouldn't be immune to it. Now, add further pressure from underneath, when everything was forcefully shifted, and it would have literally been between a rock and a hard place. No body in the universe is perfectly rigid. Anything under application of force undergoes deformation. Even a rigid body undergoes some slight change in its shape."

At the words 'change in shape' Aran perked up with understanding. "You think the tunnels have changed their shape. Enough to compress around the pods?"

"At least at that point. It obviously wasn't much, not enough for us to be able to discern it with the naked eye, but that tunnel is very carefully sculpted to be form fitting around the pods. There's barely any room on all sides to begin with. It wouldn't take much."

"But why would the tunnel only compress smaller on one part?" Aran shook his head and answered his own question. "No, of course it would. If there's two different forces applied to the rock, it won't uniformly change, the deformation will vary. The forces applied may not affect all the parts of the rock or they may not cancel each other."

One of the reasons why Sevana quite liked having Aran around was that he wasn't an idiot. She so despaired of repeating herself ad nauseum or breaking things down into layman's terms. "Precisely. This is still mostly conjecture on my part, but I'll bet my boots I'm right. We'll need to go into the tunnels tomorrow and properly measure their width and height to verify it."

His dark brow arched in a sardonic manner. "Don't give me that. You'll measure things to prove it to everyone else. You know very well that you're right."

Smirking, she patted him lightly on the cheek. "You do know me so well."

Rolling his eyes, he asked patiently, "So if nothing is wrong, can we go back to sleep? You can prove your point in the morning."

"Certainly." Sevana's hand still rested on his cheek and her heart gave a lurch at the memory of their kiss. Would it be inappropriate to initiate another one now? She wanted him to continue his affections, after all.

But no, it was late. And she didn't want to seem too forward and scare him away. As a sort of apology for waking him, she leaned up to give him a quick, chaste kiss instead. "Didn't mean to wake you up to begin with."

"I like this new way of apologizing," Aran informed her mock-gravely. "Do feel free to continue."

Snorting, she pushed him off the bed, though inwardly she felt immensely pleased with the way that had gone. "Go sleep."

Visibly amused, he did so, shuffling off back to his own bed. Sevana lay back down as well, breathing deep, trying to relax enough to fall back asleep again. It proved something of a struggle, as she could still feel Aran's lips on her own, and she was excited to prove her theory about the tunnels. Even though she couldn't trust her new magic to fix it herself just yet, it would be rewarding to give people a solution. Really, the fun part of problem-solving was unveiling the fix.

Eventually, she did fall asleep, a grin on her face as she anticipated the morning.

They went to the station early, before most people even made it out of their houses. No one was about—not that she really expected anyone at work yet—but Sevana had come prepared. She took the measuring tape out of her pocket and extended one end to Aran. With his help, they measured the mouth of the tube and got its dimensions. "Alright, we know the pod can get through here perfectly. So this is our measurement. Let's go in."

Stifling a yawn, Aran followed her in. "You owe me lunch later, you crazy woman. We could have at least grabbed something on the way here."

"Yes, yes, I'll treat you." Sevana nearly skipped ahead of him, downright perky. No doubt she'd regret skipping breakfast at some point, but she was far too excited to even think of something mundane like food now. The ocean floor was cooler in the morning, and she hugged her jacket tightly to her torso, but the temperature didn't deter her, either. She was determined to prove that she was right. She speed-walked forward, her legs eating up the ground quickly.

"For a convalescing woman, you're walking my legs off," Aran complained to her.

"After my magical core was properly switched over to Fae, I've felt much better," Sevana confided, not slowing a whit. "I'm not even achy like I usually am."

"I'd be glad to hear it if you weren't walking my legs off." He gave her a sideways roll of the eyes as Aran stretched his legs in order to keep up. "Are you absolutely sure about this theory of yours?"

Sevana slowed her pace a touch so that she could converse with him as they walked. "Almost positive. You said before that we would have seen cracks along the tunnels if there had been compression, correct? But we do see cracks."

"Not on the inside—" he objected, then paused before looking carefully around them. The damp coolness of the tunnels washed over their bare skin as they walked and Sevana could see the wheels turning. "If the tunnels compressed inwards, shrinking the passage as you suspect, it wouldn't show cracks along the interior. It would more than likely develop on the exterior, where there's room to expand."

Sevana grinned at him. Now he got the picture. "Quite. And we saw cracks on the exterior. Of course, at the time, we assumed them to be because of the slope. And some of them might still be because of the slope. I'll wager any odds you care to name that not all of them are because of that."

"It would explain why the effect is random." Aran's tone indicated he now spoke more rhetorically, half to himself. "Why it doesn't affect every tunnel, and why the area up until the reef is passable."

"And it wouldn't take much." When Sevana glanced up at him, she could see the calculations racing through his mind as he looked overhead. "An inch any direction, that's all it would take."

Silence fell for a while as they quickly walked. Sevana was personally thankful that the area to the reef wasn't that far away. She'd been grateful for that yesterday too, while waiting on a rescue, and just as much now. She rarely needed to walk anywhere these days, what with all of the vehicles that she had at her disposal.

Halfway there, she heard a shout from the other end. Stopping, they both turned, but could barely see more than a silhouette. "Is that Loman?"

"I think so. Stay here," Aran urged her. "I'll go tell him what we're doing and have him catch up with us."

She nodded agreement (truly, she didn't want to do any unnecessary hiking, as she still tired easily these days) and watched as he ran back at a ground-eating lope. For all that he complained at her pace, Sevana suspected he was mostly trying to keep her from overdoing it. Aran could run all day and not tire. Which, come to think of it, might be a Tracker's trick more than a Fae's. Or did she only feel that way because of her half-Fae body?

Standing about seemed useless so Sevana used the time to her advantage as Aran fetched the engineer. Cheating a might with Fae magic, she requested that a touch of basalt ease around the measuring tape to hold it steady as she measured the width. The answer to her early morning revelation stared right back at her as she beamed at the tape. Tunnel used to be six feet and two inches wide. Now it was an inch shy. Pods were exactly six feet wide.

Sevana cackled to herself. She did love her brain. Even if it did choose to share things at inconvenient times.

Now, the question was, did this warped section continue all the way through? She wasn't actually to the troublesome spot yet, so did this get worse further ahead?

Something made her pause. Instinct, perhaps, or…no, her Fae ears had picked up something. It was faint, a grinding noise, something like two sharp edges of rock grating against each other. It brought her head up sharply, as she'd heard that sound exactly once before in her life. When Big was being attacked by that evil magician, and chunks of rock had fallen out of him, collapsing the tunnels.

Swearing viciously to herself, she spun on a heel and raced for the entrance. Even as she moved, she heard more and more cracking noises, ominous and chilling, but worse, she could see the tunnel ceiling buckling under the pressure. A glance up confirmed a huge crack developing along the top, water squeezing through in a high-pressure spray that wet her head and shoulders as she passed under it.

The movement of the tunnel hadn't gone unnoticed by those at the other end. Aran screamed out a warning to her and she realized that he was heading back inside. That terrified her, as there was a slim chance he could reach her, and even if he did, what then? "NO!" she screamed, still running. "Don't come here!"

Loman saw sense in that, as he caught Aran's arm, pulling him sharply back. Aran fought the engineer off, or at least, Sevana thought he did. She lost the thread of what the men were doing as the rumbling crack around her became sharper, more water pouring through in a cold gusher.

The realization sent a raw wave of panic spiking through her: She wouldn't make it.

In reflex, Sevana's hands went to her belt, her pouch, reaching for a wand. A tool. But she was not a traditional Artifactor anymore, and she had nothing on her to aid herself. Heart thumping, she swallowed hard, looking about herself in terror. Either the water would drown her, or the tunnel would collapse and crush her, and Sevana didn't like either option.

Her only chance of hope was her Fae magic. Untried, unpracticed though it was. Instinctively, she called to the basalt rock around her as she had to the quartz the day before. She struggled to remember what Aran had taught her the day before: to not command, but explain what she needed, to visualize it, and let the rock do her bidding. It was strangely harder than she realized, not having to dictate every single thing, trusting the magic and the elements to respond.

There was a moment in which Sevana learned what it was like to have heart palpitations. It was not pleasant. The whole world seemed to falling apart around her, and she didn't know whether to scream or—

Then the basalt raced to her, answering the summons, wrapping around her in a hard, rocky cocoon. She folded up with her knees in her chest, eyes darting about as the rock formed. Some of the water was trapped in with her, no helping that, but the rock went solid and sank with a hard thunk to the sea floor. Outside and around her, she could hear the screams and groan as the tunnel collapsed, tearing itself apart.

Sevana held her breath, heart beating a wardrum in her ears, staying still and taut to see how this would play out. Would her round ball of rock be enough to protect her? Would the tunnel collapse on top of her, making it impossible to retrieve her out from under the mess? No, calm down, these were Fae and Unda outside. The elements would obey them, this wasn't like a human rescue, where they would need some sort of leverage to get her back out. Even now, the rock would likely be getting a scolding for daring to collapse in the first place.

"It's because of all the work they've been doing on adjusting the slope," she muttered to herself crossly. "That's why the tunnel collapsed as it did, they didn't take into account the pressure this area is already under. They just forced it back into shape without considering the consequences. It's a miracle this didn't happen days ago. Well, maybe not a miracle. A miracle wouldn't involve me getting stuck in the middle of it."

Feeling like she shouldn't just complain, Sevana tentatively patted the section of basalt under her hand. "You're a good rock. Thank you for helping me."

Was it her imagination, or did the basalt just glow for a moment, as if preening?

Peering down at that section, her mind went off on a brief flight of fancy. What if she took this chunk of basalt home with her? Would Big be jealous that she was playing with another rock that wasn't him?

Shaking the image off, her mind returned to logical, sensible worries. She'd planned on practicing magic again today, after measuring the tubes and getting an answer, but this was *not* how she and Aran had planned for the day to go. Oh mercy, Aran was likely going insane out there. For once, he couldn't come to the rescue; the water would be the perfect barrier to keep him out. He must be tearing his hair out.

Sevana sat back with a groan. For a split second, she hadn't known if she could pull herself through this disaster without being squished to death. If she made it through this—no, no, don't be foolish. She'd make it fine. *When* she made it through this, she was going to ask Aran straight out if he would like to court.

Near-death experiences were handy like that. They showed her exactly what her priorities should be. Dying with regrets was not in the plans.

The basalt rock about her moved, just a little, but forward. Had someone already uncovered her? That would be remarkable, actually, as she couldn't have been trapped down there for more than five minutes. Although the way the air turned steadily stagnant indicated that a timely rescue was indeed in order. Her cocoon shifted again, this time rolling, and she barely had time to brace her hands above her head before the whole thing rolled and turned her upside down.

Sevana's knee banged against the rock, no doubt forming a bruise, and the half-gallon of water trapped with her sloshed as she rolled. Grimacing, she braced herself better and kept her mouth and eyes firmly closed to avoid getting sea water splashed in it as she was unceremoniously rolled, gaining momentum. Yes, good, let's get this quickly over with.

The outside gave no indication of where she was in relation to the station, only the dim sounds of grating rock as she crossed over the broken tunnel. In a blink, however, she must have crossed into the air bubble near the station, as she could hear the basalt around her hit the street, and a burst of voices chattering, muted as it was through the rock.

Her cocoon split roughly in half, spilling her out of it like a chick hatching from an egg. Two strong hands that she'd know anywhere caught her by the shoulders, then she blinked up into the much brighter light and blew out a breath of relief from the fresh air.

Aran looked her over frantically before catching her up in his arms, pulling her not only free but off the ground altogether. "Thank you. Thank you for being quick on your feet and brilliant."

Bemused on how she should answer that, she hugged him back, arms around his neck and shoulders. It was an awkward angle like this, half-caught up against his chest, but Sevana had no intention of telling him so just yet. She needed a minute herself, and the grip that Aran maintained told her without words that he wasn't going to let go of her anytime soon. "Breathe, Aran. I'm alright. And look, my first real use of Fae magic went off without a hitch. It's nice basalt, really, I want to thank it. How do you thank a rock?"

A watery chuckle escaped his mouth but he didn't lift his head from where he'd hidden it in the crook of her neck. "No idea."

Another person's hand touched her shoulders and Sevana reluctantly lifted her head to glance over her shoulder. Loman looked up at her with a worried frown pulling his brows together. "You're alright?"

"Barely bruised," Sevana assured him. She patted Aran, gesturing that she wanted down, and he set her slowly on her feet but didn't let her budge an inch further. So it was going to be like that, was it? Well, alright. She could stay near him for a while longer. She could use the reassurance too, truth tell. "Loman. Did you just shove the slope back into position without considering the torque effect that would have on the tunnel?"

Loman winced. His expression said it all.

Rolling her eyes, she prayed for patience. "I'm sure that it's going to take you the rest of the day to clean that tunnel up. How about I come back out here tomorrow, help you do some stress tests, and then we can re-do the slope *properly* before rebuilding the tubes."

Hangdog, Loman nodded and gave her a sheepish smile. "We'll look forward to your guidance."

Almost as an afterthought, she tacked on, "And before that tunnel so rudely collapsed on me, I'd measured far enough in to get an answer. The rock had compressed on all sides and shrunk the interior. I'll wager it's the same case with all of the tunnels were the pods get stuck."

Enlightened, Loman turned and regarded the remaining two tubes. "Interesting. I'll measure them as well."

Aran grinned on some internal level, his eyes danced with it, but he tried to keep a straight face. "So, in other words, you're going to be perfectly insufferable the rest of the day."

"Pretty much," she agreed, still bouncing. "I do so adore it when I'm right. Which, you must admit, is most of the time."

Shaking his head, he wisely let that one pass.

Frown deepening, Loman said in a rhetorical tone, "Although considering what happened with this one, the other two have likely sustained damage."

"I honestly believe that it would easier to dismantle all of the tubes and reconstruct them," Sevana informed him factually. "With Fae magic, it shouldn't take you more than a few weeks. This station might even be up and running by the time I leave you."

"It likely will," Loman agreed, still staring thoughtfully at his tunnels. "Still, to answer the academic question, I'll examine them. Thank you, Artifactor. Our sincere apologies that you were in danger."

"It's fine," she assured him.

Aran grumbled in a hiss, "It's not."

Loman's shoulders hunched in and wisely did not address Aran's ire. "Will you update our queen and king? I have no doubt they've received the report on this and are on their way."

Sevana grimaced. Did she have to? As much as she'd like to skip that part of the process, she unfortunately couldn't. Rane had assigned her the job personally, which meant she had to report in person when she finally had the solution. Growling, she shrugged. "Fine. I'll head back and report it. I'm likely due for another treatment anyway. I'll be at the guest house the rest of the day, you can reach me there."

Loman waved her on, his attention already turning back to the project at hand.

Sevana left him to it. She needed to settle Aran first, before he worked himself up into a fine state. Catching his face with both hands, she focused his attention solely on her. "I'm fine."

He leaned in, head tilting just so, catching her mouth in a very firm and demanding kiss. Sevana, initially startled, relaxed after a moment and leaned into it. This second time kissing Aran was better than the first, likely because she knew what to expect this time, and it was hard not to smile as their lips slid and caressed each other's. Aran pulled back after several long, quite pleasant moments, resting their foreheads together. "I love you, Sevana, so please. I'm begging you. No more near-death experiences. My heart can't take it."

Loved her? She blinked, then pulled back enough to study his face, searching, although she wasn't sure for what. Aran loved her. Sevana had always known he loved her, but she didn't suspect it to be *this* kind of love, not until this moment. The knowledge lit her up, the force of her joy so intense that she felt as if she had a second sun trying to burst out of her chest. And it was such an amazing relief, as well, that he felt the same for her. Sevana really had no idea how she would have seduced him; seeing that it was no longer necessary was vastly reassuring.

Perhaps the relief made her giddy, as she didn't think anything of popping up on her toes in a public place and kissing him again, lips lingering. She felt shy saying it, and strangely awkward, as sentiment always made her feel out of joint. But still, she owed him the words. She owed them both the words. "I love you too."

A blinding smile crossed over his face, and he closed in the distance to kiss her again, tenderly this time. Sevana really did like this kissing business.

They might have kept going in this vein except someone passing by wolf-whistled, and someone else snickered, which brought Sevana sharply back to reality. Right, they were standing outside of the station, weren't they? Heat flooded her cheeks as she drew back, settling onto her heels once more.

Aran took the teasing in stride and shooed people on their way. "Yes, yes, show's over. Off with you."

"Well." Clearing her throat, Sevana looked carefully elsewhere, trying to yank the blush off her face with limited success. When that failed, she caught his arm and started towing them for the guest house. "That let the cat out of the bag."

Matching her pace, he inquired, "What do you mean?"

"Well, after that sort of display, people will think we're…" she trailed off, belatedly realizing that she hadn't properly asked if they could court. Although with their mutual declaration of affections, surely that was a given?

"Courting, yes. I don't think it's news to anyone." Aran stopped short and frowned down at her. "Did you want to keep that secret?"

"What?" Sevana stared back at him dumbly, striving to ignore the pounding in her chest and the swooping butterflies swarming about in her stomach. "I—I thought—" actually, voicing what she had thought seemed so spectacularly stupid that she couldn't manage to spit out the words. "We're courting?"

He stared at her hard, as if she had become this enigmatic puzzle to solve. "How could you possibly ask that after…wait. Were you not paying any attention while I was talking to you that first day I kissed you?"

"What? When?" Sevana looked up, narrowing her eyes and searching her memory. She'd been studying the schematics and reading the history log, and Aran had been going on about something that he seemed to think was serious, and she'd made the right noises at the appropriate intervals, all while thinking about the problem at hand. And then the kissing started, and Sevana had genuinely paid attention for that part.

"Great magic, you weren't. You really weren't listening to a word I said." Aran rubbed a hand over his forehead and huffed out a disbelieving laugh. "For gods' sake, Sevana, you carried on a conversation! I told you that I was completely, utterly in love with you and asked if we could court, and you said that was alright, fine, and you very sweetly kissed me!"

Sevana stared, wide-eyed, as this new piece of information fell into place. She was aware that she was probably expected to say something, but her brain and mouth seemed not to be cooperating with each other just then.

"Wait a minute. I know what I was doing, but what were *you* doing?"

"I was trying not to do anything that would make you want to stop doing, you know," she flapped her hands in irritation, not knowing words to use, "things!" Sevana blurted. She shuffled her weight from one foot to the other. "You're not going to stop, are you? I'd prefer things to keep going as they have been."

Aran stared at her, perfectly incredulous for what seemed like a small eternity, before dissolving into an undignified fit of snickering. "For someone so brilliant, you can be such an idiot."

She should probably be offended by that, but Sevana unfortunately really didn't have a leg to stand on.

16

Another two weeks passed. With her magical core now settled, it was easier to tackle the rest of her body. The muscles, bones, tendons and other internal organs were all subtly changed to be stronger and less inclined to deteriorate than a human body. Her mind was changed a little as well, now able to better accept the input from the senses, and that was by far the most delicate part of the process. Ursilla did not rush that as she had everything else, instead putting a day in between each treatment until Sevana's brain was entirely adapted over to Fae.

Sevana was grateful for that, as that rash of treatments had left her with a throbbing migraine and she'd definitely needed time to recoup in between.

Still, that aside, the daily treatments with Aran and Ursilla went much smoother than they had in the beginning, no longer leaving Sevana in a Gordian knot of weird side effects. She still tired after the treatments, and sometimes her body ran hot or cold, but that was all bearable compared to before.

As she recovered, Loman dutifully tested and measured all of the tunnels, finding—to no one's surprise—that all of the tunnels giving them trouble were two inches smaller than before. What with the trouble they'd already experienced, no one was willing to risk a repeat. Sevana went out herself with the crews, at least when she was physically up to it, and either examined the work that they did or put her new magic to use by helping them level and rebuild the tubes from scratch.

It strangely felt natural to her to work with the Fae magic, more so than her human magic had been. As an Artifactor, Sevana had constantly struggled to make the magic do as she wished, and spent far more time working out the mathematical properties and logistics of something on paper than actually performing magic itself. Doing things now was simplicity itself in comparison—although she still did a fair share of calculating.

A week before she was due to be done with her treatments, the tunnels were in operation again for the first time in two decades. The city under the waves had a grand party to celebrate it, re-blessing the station with a very elaborate ritual that Curano and Rane oversaw. Sevana attended part of it, but she wasn't much for parties, and used an excuse of feeling tired to escape early.

On the morning of the final day of her treatment, she rose and packed everything into her single bag. All of Master and Sarsen's 'gifts' (bribes, more like it) had already been shipped ahead to Big, thankfully. The idea of lugging three crates full of things with her made Sevana glad she'd thought ahead and bought it all well before this point. With her things packed, she looked about the room, mentally going through a checklist. Only the final treatment was left. Really, there was very little of her that was human; the final treatment was more like a final pass to make sure nothing human remained. Ursilla thought her done. This was a 'just in case' measure and nothing more. Because of that, Sevana planned to return to Nopper's Woods today.

If she never saw another fish or clam, it would be too soon.

Aran poked his head around the door. "Ursilla will be here in a moment. I vote we leave immediately after she's done and have a late breakfast on land."

"It's like you read minds," Sevana agreed in relief. "I can't take another bowl of fishy."

"Ditto." A quick grin flashed over his face before he ducked away again.

Bacon. Bacon was definitely on her agenda. And biscuits. Jam. Rubbing her hands together in anticipation, she took a good look around the room. Rane had generously outfitted her for her stay here, and Sevana wanted to keep everything given to her and not offend her hostess. She went around to all the rooms, making sure she hadn't forgotten something, and did spy a few odds and ends that had to be stuck into the bag. Satisfied she'd gotten it all, she firmly pressed the last thing in to make sure the strap could come over and actually buckle into place. It took more than a little strength and determination to make that happen, as the strap strained to make it to the first hole and allow her to buckle it in place.

"Sellion!" Ursilla called from the main room.

Funny how more and more people called her by her Fae name as her transformation took place. It was as if the more she shed her human blood, the more they felt it appropriate to call her only as the Fae did. Sevana couldn't entirely disagree with this attitude, as she no longer felt as herself. Her body felt stronger, lighter, and far more in tune with the world around her than she had as a human. Her senses were far sharper as well. The energies of the world lay visible to her eyes in a way that she'd never experienced before, even with the aid of all of her magical tools.

It had been a rough road getting to this point, but now that Sevana was fully Fae in body and magic, she had to admit that it wasn't unpleasant. Gaining her current status had been well worth the journey.

Shouldering her pack, a small smile played around her mouth as she came to stand in front of Ursilla. The elderly Unda eyed her critically from head to toe and back again, dark eyes making an evaluating sweep before she gave a grudging nod. "I thought another treatment might be in order, but it seems that your Fae magic has awakened enough to do the job for me. There's nothing left of your humanity."

"I disagree," Sevana responded, smile becoming enigmatic. "I still retain a human's knowledge, don't I? And experience."

"Yes," the Unda acknowledged, sharing that enigmatic smile. "You are the only one living to do so, I believe. It will be very interesting what you choose to do with that adult human knowledge as Fae."

Sevana snorted. "I would think that's obvious." When she got twin looks from both Aran and Ursilla, her tone went very dry. "Really, you two. I'm an Artifactor. Just because I'm Fae now doesn't change that. I'll need to practice with my Fae magic, maybe study for a year or so until I get a grasp on what I can do, but I'm perfectly sure that I can still work."

Ursilla spluttered, flabbergasted. "But you won't need to!"

"Just because I was down for the count, do you really think the work went away?" Sevana demanded of her, exasperated. "You think people stopped being cursed, that evil magicians ceased doing evil? Come now, Ursilla, you know that isn't the case. I wasn't popular as an Artifactor just because I was a prodigy, you know. I was popular because I was *effective.* People knew they could retain me and actually get the problem solved."

Aran tapped a thoughtful finger to his lips. "I know you said before that you would still want to go out and about the world, but I assumed you would be working on your own projects."

"And so I will. But I've always worked on my own projects while waiting for challenging cases to come to me." Sevana shrugged, as she thought that obvious. "Nothing much has changed."

Aran's eyebrows rose, although he seemed less surprised and more calculating. "You really think you can use Fae magic to create magical artifacts as you did before?"

"Why not?" she challenged.

Mouth curling up, he murmured, "Why not, indeed. I really shouldn't underestimate your determination. If anyone can figure out how to do it, you can. Well, Ursilla, if you see no need for a further treatment, we'll be on our way."

Ursilla did not say anything for a moment, her head cocked in question as she studied Sevana a moment longer. "Write to me," she finally said—practically ordered. "Let me know how you are doing. I wish to see how you develop from here."

No doubt for the woman's own records and curiosity, but Sevana didn't mind that. She would feel the same way if their roles were reversed. "I will."

"Good luck," Ursilla offered, stepping aside to let them pass her. "Artifactor."

Grinning at the woman, Sevana shouldered her pack once more. "Thank you, Ursilla. Truly, thank you for all your help."

"You are very welcome." Ursilla watched from the doorway as they walked past her.

Sevana had said most of her goodbyes the day before, as she didn't expect to be in this corner of the world again anytime soon. Loman had thanked her profusely, promising he'd call her first the next time they had a problem they couldn't solve. Sevana laughingly promised to come, too, if that ever happened. Still, despite saying her goodbyes, she wasn't in the least surprised to find Rane and Curano waiting for them. Someone had to take them safely to the surface, true enough, but this was hardly the task for a queen or king.

Curano wore his loose-fitting kilt of dark purple and nothing else except twin gold bracelets around both ankles. The Unda king regarded her seriously with his dark blue eyes but did not speak. Sevana had learned in her time down here that he wasn't much of a talker. He seemed to leave most of that up to his wife.

Rane looked resplendent, as normal, in her choice of flowing dress, a pure white this time, her dark hair in an elaborate braid over one shoulder that was strung with pearls and shells. She had a slight pout on her face as they approached her. "You can stay longer, you know."

"No, I really can't," Sevana denied, barely resisting the urge to roll her eyes. Rane had not entirely given up on the idea of keeping her, it seemed. "I have things to do up there, and if I delay any longer, I'll have a drag-out fight with Aranhil about me living in Big. The man's already threatened to move me out no matter what my opinion. I'd better nip that in the bud."

"But you will come back and see us," Rane demanded, arms still crossed over her chest.

"Yes, yes. I won't go into South Woods yet. I still have things to do in the human world. And yes, before you ask, if I find any more orphans I'll bring them to you."

That satisfied her. At least, it did the trick long enough for her to pull in an air bubble around them and finally escort them toward the surface. Curano only waved them off. He didn't intend to see them all the way up, then? Just a farewell. That suited Sevana fine.

Sevana felt mostly relieved to finally escape the dark depths of the ocean, but she couldn't help but glance back once at the city that had sheltered her for nearly two months. It grew smaller and smaller in the distance as they left it, and for all that she was ready to go home, she felt a spark of gratitude to the place. It had done well by her, and Sevana would remember that.

They breached the waves at last, and the air bubble around them dissipated with a pop, allowing a cool sea breeze to rush over them, rustling her hair and clothing. Sevana drew in her first clear breath of air with a smile on her face. The cold water still lapped around her ankles—they weren't free of the water just yet—but the sun felt good against her skin. It was like a homecoming, being on the surface once more.

Because she'd expected to come home today, she'd written both Master and Aranhil, informing them of such, and they timed it so they were on the shore waiting on her. Master she expected, and Aranhil, but not Kip, Bel, and Sarsen. For that matter, Grydon and Baby had been lounging on the beach sand until her appearance, and they promptly leapt up and tackled her with wagging tails and insistent head bumps until she got free of the water and was able to kneel down and give them a good scratch.

"Well," she said brightly to the waiting men. "This is quite the welcome party."

Bel went directly for her and scooped her up, hugging her hard. "I'm so glad you came through that in one piece."

"Yes, yes," she said impatiently, trying to push him off. "There's no call for hugs."

Laughing, he hugged her tighter. "And I'm glad to see that you haven't changed, not really." Stepping back, he looked her over, noticing the minute differences. Her ears had changed, elongating, eyes becoming more cat-like in the pupils, body slightly thicker with muscle. "You look healthier than ever. I'm glad."

"Not as much as we are," Aran assured the human king. "Trust me on that. Aranhil, I've returned with your daughter."

It was a very formal phrasing and Aranhil inclined his head in acceptance. "You have, and have done well. We thank you. Rane, you have sheltered my daughter in her time of need. You have my thanks."

Rane gave him a pretty smile, head tilted in a falsely demure way. "You're quite welcome. She is always welcome to come, for that matter."

The look Aranhil gave her neatly conveyed that he understood what she really meant by that and he wasn't having it. Ignoring the jibe, he squeezed past Bel and got his own hug in, thankfully brief, before making a show of looking Sevana over. "You do look well, daughter. I'm very pleased by that."

Master, impatient with all of the others hogging her, came in from behind to give her a back hug. "You do look well, sweetling, but I'm avidly curious and have a million questions. What you wrote to me was too dry and factual, I need more details."

Catching Sarsen's and Kip's eyes, she asked dryly, "You two feel the same way, I take it?"

"Of course." Kip looked at her as if she had just asked a very stupid question.

"Breakfast," Sevana demanded of them all. "I need breakfast, and I'll answer questions. Although, really, Aran knows more than I do in some ways. My eyes weren't up to the task in the beginning."

"That's fine." Master gestured toward his land carriage sitting nearby—a larger version that was obviously meant to hold this many people. Well, that explained how they all got here, anyway. "I can think of a place nearby that serves a quite excellent breakfast. Would you care to join us, Rane?"

"I cannot," Rane said regretfully. Her tone did not match the mischief in her eyes. "But I thank you for the invitation. Sevana, Arandur, I hope to see you again soon. I wish you happiness in your courtship, and if you do decide to Handfast, do tell me. I want to attend the ceremony."

Oh she did *not*. Sevana didn't growl at her, although it came close.

"Courtship?" several voices chorused at once, some of them incredulous, others delighted. To be precise, Aranhil, Master and Sarsen were delighted, Kip and Bel were incredulous.

With a little wave of the fingers, Rane skipped back to the water's edge and dove neatly into the waves.

Sevana shared a speaking look with Aran. "Why do we like her, again?"

Chuckling, Aran shrugged. He didn't seem the least bothered that Rane had just stolen their thunder. "She has her moments. Yes, everyone, we're courting. Have been for several weeks now. We wanted to tell you in person, and yes, that's something else we will talk about over breakfast. Everyone into the carriage, now, we're starving for proper food."

"Bacon," Sevana chimed in, tone brisk and allowing no nonsense as she pushed her way through bodies toward the carriage. "Biscuits. I accept nothing less than that."

"Wait, Sevana," Bel scurried to keep up with her, "are you and Arandur really going to Handfast?"

"We're courting; we haven't talked about that yet." Although Sevana had every intention of doing so. "Breakfast, Bel, focus."

"But what about being an Artifactor?" Sarsen asked at her other elbow, taking her sack from her to help secure it into the boot at the back. "Now that you're Fae, you surely won't—why are you looking at me like I just asked a stupid question?"

"It is a stupid question," she retorted tartly. "Really, you think I can just laze about South Woods for the next several centuries and be happy without something to intellectually challenge me? You, of all people, know what I'm like when I'm bored."

Sarsen's eyes sharpened on hers. "But a Fae Artifactor?"

"Why not?" she challenged, standing her ground.

Looking entirely flummoxed by the idea, he stared at her for a long moment before, oddly, turning to Aran. "And what do you think of this?"

"That I'm not stupid enough to tell her what she can and cannot do." Arandur stared him down. "Since when has Sevana ever let the conventional cage her?"

Deciding that Sarsen's brain had been scrambled by the surprise—it had to have been, if he was asking stupid questions—she ignored him utterly and climbed in. When no one else immediately did so, she popped her head around the doorway and enunciated clearly: "Bacon."

Chuckling, Master clambered inside. "Yes, yes, sweetling. We'll feed you. It'll take a half hour or so to reach the restaurant I'm thinking of. Why don't you start answering a few questions as we go? Come on, everyone, don't stand there waiting."

With no sense of decorum or rank, every man piled in, finding their own seats. Sevana was idly curious on how two kings managed to get here without any sort of entourage. Well, no, that might be a stupid question too. Master wouldn't think anything of swinging by and casually kidnapping two monarchs. Nor would either of these men think anything of just climbing in to go pick her up from the Unda.

It did please her, to have them here. She'd come through a milestone, and part of her wanted to share in the joy of that. She looked around at all of their faces, all of them so eagerly waiting to hear from her, and her heart strings tugged from happiness. "Well. Where shall I start?"

The Fae Artifactor

Legend says that there was once a human Artifactor, a prodigy in her field. She was called upon by kings, by the Fae, by the gods themselves. She excelled in curse-breaking but used her talents in other ways, preventing disasters and rescuing the ones most desperate for help. One legend says that she even prevented Nanashi Isle from being destroyed by a volcano, although many believe that one to be something of an exaggeration.

She was so loved by magic, so gifted in her talents, that even the Fae envied her. They took her as a daughter, changed her magic and form, making her Fae in truth. Some say that she even married another Fae, a dark-haired Tracker who followed her faithfully wherever she went.

People have claimed to see her throughout the centuries. When kings are in trouble, when even the gods are beside themselves, they call upon her. The Fae Artifactor still comes and solves their problems, breaks their curses, unravels their mysteries. It's said that even now, three hundred years after her rebirth as Fae, she still walks in the human world and works the mysteries of magic.

It might be legend, it might be truth, but if you go to the edge of Nopper's Woods and find the talking mountain, they say that you can call upon her. They say the mountain will relay your request to her, the Fae Artifactor.

They say that even now, she'll come.

To all of the fans who love and adore Artifactor–

It's been something of a ride in this series, hasn't it? I admit that I started *The Child Prince* with the vague idea of a snarky character that solved magical mysteries and not much else. It was fun to write Sevana. She said aloud the tempting thing at the wrong (or right) moments, was an unapologetic brat, and yet she moved the world for people when it needed to be moved. She'll always be near and dear to me.

You'll likely see her pop up again from time to time, like in the Christmas short stories, so don't despair that this is the end of her story completely. But this is definitely the last official book of the *Artifactor* series. Thanks for all the love, support, whining, begging, and cheers for this cast of characters.

See you in the next world –

Dear Reader,

Your reviews are very important. Reviews directly impact sales and book visibility, and the more reviews we have, the more sales we see. The more sales there are, the longer I get to keep writing the books you love full time. The best possible support you can provide is to give an honest review, even if it's just clicking those stars to rate the book!

Thank you for all your support! See you in the next world.

~Honor

Honor Raconteur is a sucker for a good fantasy. Despite reading it for decades now, she's never grown tired of the magical world. She likely never will.
In between writing books, she trains and plays with her dogs, eats far too much chocolate, and attempts insane things like aerial dance.

If you'd like to join her newsletter to be notified when books are released, and get behind the scenes about upcoming books, you can isit her website or email directly to honorraconteur.news@raconteurhouse.com and you'll be added to the mailing list. If you'd like to interact with Honor more directly, you can socialize with her on various sites. Each platform offers something different and fun!

Other books by Honor Raconteur
Published by Raconteur House

♫ Available in Audiobook! ♫

THE ADVENT MAGE CYCLE

Jaunten ♫
Magus ♫
Advent ♫
Balancer ♫

ADVENT MAGE NOVELS
Advent Mage Compendium
The Dragon's Mage ♫
The Lost Mage

WARLORDS (ADVENT MAGE)

Warlords Rising
Warlords Ascending
Warlords Reigning

THE ARTIFACTOR SERIES

The Child Prince ♫
The Dreamer's Curse ♫
The Scofflaw Magician
The Canard Case
The Fae Artifactor

THE CASE FILES OF HENRI DAVENFORTH

Magic and the Shinigami Detective
Charms and Death and Explosions (oh my)

DEEPWOODS SAGA

Deepwoods ♪
Blackstone
Fallen Ward

Origins

FAMILIAR AND THE MAGE

The Human Familiar
The Void Mage
Remnants
Echoes

GÆLDORCRÆFT FORCES

Call to Quarters

KINGMAKERS

Arrows of Change ♪
Arrows of Promise
Arrows of RevolutionKINGSLAYER

Kingslayer ♪
Sovran at War ♪

SINGLE TITLES

Special Forces 01
Midnight Quest

Crossroads: An Artifactor x Deepwoods Crossover Short Story

Printed in Great Britain
by Amazon